Barry Crump wrote his fi
Man, in 1960. It became
numerous other books wh
famous and best-loved New Zealand character is Sam
Cash, who features in *Hang on a Minute Mate*,
Crump's second book. Between them, these two
books have sold over 400,000 copies and continue to
sell at an amazing rate some 30 years later.

Crump began his working life as a professional
hunter, culling deer and pigs in some of the ruggedest
country in New Zealand. After the runaway success
of his first book, he pursued many diverse
activities, including goldmining, radio talkback,
white-baiting, television presenting, crocodile
shooting and acting.

As to classifying his occupation, Crump always
insisted that he was a Kiwi bushman.

He published 25 books and was awarded the MBE for
services to literature in 1994.

Books by Barry Crump

A Good Keen Man (1960)
Hang on a Minute Mate (1961)
One of Us (1962)
There and Back (1963)
Gulf (1964) – now titled *Crocodile Country*
Scrapwaggon (1965)
The Odd Spot of Bother (1967)
No Reference Intended (1968)
Warm Beer and Other Stories (1969)
A Good Keen Girl (1970)
Bastards I Have Met (1970)
Fred (1972)
Shorty (1980)
Puha Road (1982)
The Adventures of Sam Cash (1985)
Wild Pork and Watercress (1986)
Barry Crump's Bedtime Yarns (1988)
Bullock Creek (1989)
The Life and Times of a Good Keen Man (1992)
Gold and Greenstone (1993)
Arty and the Fox (1994)
Forty Yarns and a Song (1995)
Mrs Windyflax and the Pungapeople (1995)
Crumpy's Campfire Companion (1996)
As the Saying Goes (1996)
A Tribute to Crumpy: Barry Crump 1935–1996 is an anthology of tributes, extracts from Crump's books, letters and pictures from his private photo collection.

All titles currently (1997) in print.

ONE OF US

BARRY CRUMP

ONE OF US

Illustrated by Dennis Turner

Hodder Moa Beckett

I'd like to have put the Bovo Poem in the front here because in spite of what's happened I reckon that under different circumstances he could have been quite a significant sort of a bloke, but he's still working on it.

Ray Richards gave me a lot of help with getting this blasted thing written. He's a good bloke really.

It's about time I thanked Dennis Turner for the illustrations he has provided for each of my books. The yarns wouldn't have been the same without them. He's a beaut.

ISBN 1-86958-578-X

© 1962 Barry Crump

First edition 1962
Reprints numerous
This edition 1994
Reprinted 1997

Published by Hodder Moa Beckett Publishers Limited
[a member of the Hodder Headline Group]
4 Whetu Place, Mairangi Bay, Auckland, New Zealand

Cover Photo: NZPL/J Carnemolla

Printed by McPherson's Printing Group, Australia

All rights reserved. No part of this publication may be reproduced or transmitted in any form or by any means, electronic or mechanical, including photocopying, recording, or any information storage and retrieval system, without permission in writing from the publisher.

Contents

Sam . . . And Ponto	9
Shai's Yarn	21
Dan's Yarn	29
Four Pounds Ten	39
Men At Work	53
Hospitality	63
Toddy	73
Toddy In Trouble	83
T. Burke	93
West Coast Pub	97
On Contract	109
An Inside Job	123
Crook Boots	131
Pay Sam and Ponto	143
Heading North	155
The Last Drink	165
One Of Us	173
Got A Light On You, Mate?	179

Sam . . . and Ponto

Sam Cash threw a dirty look in the general direction of heaven and went into a doorway to go through his pockets, checking up on what he had. Thirty-seven bob and a nearly-empty packet of tobacco. Then he went into a pub to see if anything was going to happen.

It was an old wooden place, cool and dark and dirty. A good fire trap. Burn like the last armful of wood on a wet night, once she got going.

"I'll try an eight," he said to the only-just-sober barman in a dirty shirt and a bad humour.

Two pools of beer and a broken stool along the bar from him stood a bloke who'd had a fair bit to do with racehorses in his time by the look of him. Hand wrapped around a five-ounce glass and a *Best Bets* look on his face. Dreaming up a winner for next Saturday; or wondering where he was going to get the money to back it with. Just beyond him leaned a lumpy old overcoat with a lumpy old hat on the top and a glass of beer going flat in front of it.

Across the other side was a piebald old bloke who was going to recite "Dangerous Dan McGrew" right through when he had enough beer on board and someone would listen. With him was a pensioned-off wharfie or something who was dodging the shout and making a mess on the bar with a packet of Park Drive, from which he was rolling fat cigarettes and sucking wet ends on them.

Sam ordered another beer and looked across to where a dairy-farmer type—sharemilker, most probably—was enthusiastically entertaining an obvious bludger, spending money in the way of a man who isn't used to cutting loose. Behind him on the wall there was a worn-out dart board, a chalky blackboard and a lavatory-seat championship shield.

A trembling hand darted out from the lumpy old overcoat and clutched the drink in front of it like a magnet. Sam turned away, finished his drink and went out into the street again.

Rotten-looking bunch. Have to get the hell out of the city before a bloke ends up one of them. Need a mate though. A man can't go roaming around on his own without being noticed. And Sam didn't particularly want to be noticed just then.

He leaned against a building watching the faces of the men and the figures of the girls who were going past. After a while he gave up looking at the girls.

Scatterbrained bunch of heifers.

Then he gave up looking at the men too.

A man'd go a long way to find a mate among that dozy-looking pack. More individuals in a mob of Romney wethers.

He rolled a smoke and hoped the something that was going to happen would happen soon. Otherwise he'd have to do something about it and it wouldn't be the same.

"Got a light on you, mate?"

What the hell's this scrawny coot coming at? Can't he see a man's just lighting a smoke!

"Yeah."

He lit the crumpled tailor-made the little bloke had been holding in his mouth too long and looked at him.

Hard up, he decided. Shaved in the dark—or with a hangover—with an old blade two or three days ago. Fluff on his pants where he's been sleeping in them. Shoes in good nick but not laced up properly.

"Nice day."

"Yeah," said Sam in a way that neither agreed nor disagreed with him.

"Care for a drink?"

Sam looked at him again. Probably a bludger. What the hell anyway.

"Yeah, okay." He turned down the street away from the pub he'd just been in and the little bloke fell in beside him.

"There's not a bad boozer on the corner down here."

"Good, that'll do us," said Sam carelessly.

The little bloke, half running to keep up, dashed ahead like a small boy to open the door of the pub for Sam in an elaborate gesture of courtesy.

Crawler, decided Sam.

"What'll y' have?" asked the little bloke, producing a healthy fistful of notes from the inside pocket of his coat.

"Just a beer," said Sam, placing his folded arms on the bar.

The little sod must be a thief too.

"Two eights," said the little bloke to the barman.

It was still too early for the place to be busy. All chrome and bottles. Place was probably swarming with collars and ties later in the afternoon; all talking baloney about import restrictions and last year's holidays. Sam raised his glass and drank an inch and a half of beer. The little bloke followed his example but drank the whole glassful without swallowing.

An alcoholic!

"Not a bad drop the Waitemata crowd turns out these days."

"Not bad," agreed Sam grudgingly, gulping the rest of his beer.

He'll probably sink a few quick ones and get all matey and a man'll have a hell of a job getting rid of him.

Sam paid for the next drink.

"I should've gone back on the ferry last night," said the little bloke, with a roguish grin at the sight of Sam's disinterested face. "Got a bit of a sheep-run in the Sounds. One of my blokes was going to meet me with the launch."

"Yeah?"

Lying little coot.

"Yeah. But I ran into a little sort in the back bar of the Dominion last night and decided to stick around," he chuckled. "It was worth it too."

One more round, decided Sam, and I'll drop this sexo off and see what I can do about getting out of town.

The little bloke fished two cigarettes out of his pocket and handed one to Sam. Then he slapped his pockets and located a box of matches. He saw Sam glaring at him and stopped in the act of striking a light.

"Thought you didn't have any matches," said Sam.

The little bloke gave a half-shy, half-cheeky grin, struck the match and held it up to Sam's smoke.

"Well I had matches," he admitted. "But I didn't have anyone to have a beer with."

Sam's first real laugh in eighteen months was a bit rusty and out-of-condition.

It'd be a waste of time describing how Ponto and Sam were helped up the gangway of the Picton ferry just before it sailed that night, but I can tell you what happened when they made their feeble way ashore at Picton in the early hours of the following morning, groping and groaning, one behind the other, the roaring of the bars they'd been in the day before still ringing in their ears. One tall thin bloke sloping along in front of a short square one, both bare-headed, bloodshot and cold. They walked up the wharf in the lights of cars hurrying past toward cups of tea and warm beds. Sam didn't care and Ponto didn't notice.

Ponto, after an elaborate inspection of a little jetty to which two dinghies and a small yacht were moored, announced that the launch wasn't there to meet them.

"They must have given you up as a bad job," said Sam.

"We'll ring up when it gets light enough for them to come over."

"What's about the time?"

"Must be getting on for three."

"Then we've got about four hours to wait," said Sam.

"Yeah," said Ponto looking at the sky. "We'd better look

round for somewhere out of the wind. It's not going to get any warmer."

"Been raining," observed Sam.

"It's always raining round here this time of year."

The night was like a tin roof full of holes, with the cloudy skeleton of a storm spinning north on a wind straight off the snow. It had been raining heavily by the look of it and every few minutes it was changing from obviously-going-to-rain to obviously-not-going-to. Sam wasn't nearly as interested in the weather as he was in being out of the city and Ponto was preoccupied with something else.

They sat with their backs against a wall looking along the shivering river of light across the water to where the ferry, glowing like a heater, was plugged in. They rolled smokes and lit them.

"They reckon you never get to know a bloke till you've been on the bash with him," said Ponto too loudly.

"I suppose that's right enough in a way," agreed Sam. "But I reckon it's a lot of baloney about drunk people always telling the truth. You're more likely to get a line of bull out of a man with a skinful than when he's sober."

"Yeah, I know."

"For instance, even us. I bet we were having each other on a bit there yesterday."

"You mean in that pub where they wouldn't let us sing?"

Sam felt Ponto squirm uneasily in the dark beside him.

"Yeah."

"You mean about my farm?"

"Not exactly, Ponto. I was thinking about me telling you I shore four hundred rams a day with my wrist in plaster when I was still going to school. As a matter of fact the best day I ever done in my life was three fifty-eight, and they were all hoggets."

"Aw—I know what it's like, Sam," said Ponto eagerly. "As a matter of fact I did my share of exaggerating too—about my farm and things."

"Yeah?"

"Yeah. I think I said something about it being two thousand acres, didn't I?"

"Four thousand, actually," corrected Sam.

"Well it's a bit smaller than that."

"How much smaller?"

"Well there's about a hundred acres altogether. It's not all broken in, mind you, but I've been doing a bit on it. Got about forty acres in grass—or thirty, anyway." Ponto was talking in the quick running way of someone who's been caught at something.

"You'd have a bit of a job dragging twenty-five bales of wool twice a year off a place that size," said Sam.

Ponto didn't answer and after a while Sam went on, "Just goes to show you, doesn't it. There's no telling what a bloke's going to say once he gets started. That bit about me being a topdressing pilot wasn't all that terrible true either."

"Wasn't it?" said Ponto, obviously surprised.

"No, not exactly. I've been up in an Auster once or twice though."

"Ah well, it just goes to show."

"Sure does."

A wicked little wind with nothing better to do sniffed out the two men and shoved its hand down the back of Ponto's neck. He rattled and rustled in the wet dark, stood up, did something with his coat and sat down again.

"Y'know Sam, I think I might just have mentioned something about my farm being freehold."

"Yeah, something like that."

"Well, it's not really; there's another bloke tied up in it."

"Yeah? Who?"

"Bloke who owns the place."

"I see," said Sam casually. "Then you're just managing it for him?"

"Well—not exactly. As a matter of fact I only work there."

"In that case I don't think I'll bother taking that job as head shepherd you offered me," said Sam good-humouredly. "I haven't really got my dogs and saddle arriving from up the East Coast next week anyway."

"Now I come to think of it, I don't think he wants a shepherd just now after all," said Ponto. "There's only about fifty sheep and I think he can manage them on his own. I'd almost forgotten about that."

"What've you been doing over there?" asked Sam.

"Land development," replied Ponto; then, sensing Sam's glance, he amended it to "Scrubcutting."

"Does he want another scrubcutter then?"

"I don't think he even wants the one he's got," admitted Ponto. "In fact, I was thinking of not going back. Y'see he told me if I wasn't there to meet the launch not to bother coming back."

"Must be a tough coot to work for."

"Yeah, a real bullock-driver. Works a man like a bloody slave and pays him a lousy six-ten an acre. A bit miserable with the tucker too."

"He wouldn't be worth working for," announced Sam.

"No, I don't know why I stayed there as long as I did. I could have been making good dough all the time I wasted over there."

"How long were you there?"

"Three weeks."

"What are you going to do about your gear?"

"There's only my boots and odd bits of stuff. Not worth bothering with."

"Does he owe you anything?"

"No. I got a progress cheque off him when I went into town."

"Well in that case there's nothing to go back for—except that brand-new bulldozer of yours."

There was no need for Ponto to answer that one.

"What now?" asked Sam after a while.

"Well I was just thinking," said Ponto slowly. "You know

that brother of mine I told you about? The one with the farm just out of Murchison?"

"Yeah," said Sam carefully.

"Well, I have got a brother with a farm down there; but I think it's a bit further out than I said."

"How much further?"

"About fifty miles."

"What about it?"

"He'd give us a job like a shot, I think. It'd be worth a look."

"I've got nothing better to do," said Sam slowly. "How do we get there?"

"Hitch-hike. I've got a few quid left but we'll save that in case we miss out on the job."

There was no "in case" about it. Ponto's brother would never have let him get within rifle-shot of his place. But Ponto wasn't the type to worry about things like that until they happened. Sam had already made allowances for more than just missing out on the job so neither of them was going to be any worse off than he already was.

Broken bush skylines wrote themselves against the sky as the frayed glassy light of a September dawn discovered the valley. Then, quite suddenly, the sun was bleeding on a ridge-top behind them.

"It's getting light," said Sam.

Ponto shivered and grunted. "And bloody cold," he added.

"Never mind," said Sam cheerfully. "Looks like we're going to get a fine day out of it. We'll be able to get going shortly."

The sun rested on top of the hill for a while, looking across the sound. Then it got in behind a thick bulkhead of coffin-coloured cloud that came from nowhere and stayed there all day.

Sam stood up, stretched his long self twice all round and brushed his clothes roughly with his hands.

"Sun's got a bit of a black eye," he said. "But I don't think it's going to rain."

Ponto stood awkwardly with his hands on his knees, like an old pair of pliers that haven't been used for a long time.

"Race you round the block for a fiver," offered Sam, patting him on the shoulder and nearly knocking him over.

"Go to hell," said Ponto.

"Come on, man! Anyone'd think you were an old bloke. You don't look a day over forty-five."

Ponto didn't appreciate the joke. "I'm thirty-three, if you want to know," he snarled. "And you can't expect a joker to spend a night like that and then do acrobatics first thing in the morning."

"You must be muscle-bound," joked Sam. "I could give you a good five years. Let's find a water-tap. I'm as dry as a city pub on Sunday."

After a few minutes Ponto got his starched knees working and his temper back. They had a drink of water from a tap in a dressing-shed and walked through the town toward the south.

Shai's Yarn

THE EARLY MORNING SUNLIGHT shone through Ponto's big ears and lit them up like a pair of late-model tail-lights. Behind him Sam was transferring some tobacco into his pocket from the pocket of Ponto's coat hanging on the door of the shed they'd slept in. Ponto hadn't got much sleep. He'd sat huddled in a corner, shaking like a dog on a river bank all night. Sam had squatted by the door smoking and thinking and dozing on and off.

They were somewhere north of Murchison. How far neither of them was certain, though they'd agreed it was something between twenty and a hundred and fifty miles.

It was a half-fine morning, with bush all round and the raining-on-leaves sound of a creek somewhere nearby or a big river in the distance. Ponto was sitting in a clump of fern on the bank above the road brooding.

"That's definitely the last time I'm sleeping on the ground," he complained in a voice as stiff as his knees. "It's no bloody good to a man my age. I'll end up getting rheumatism or something and have to retire. And I'm hungry," he added.

Sam leaned against the wall of the hut watching the way Ponto's ears wiggled as he talked. Not getting an answer to what wasn't really a question anyway, Ponto turned to Sam and said, "Do you know where this road leads to?"

"Well, there's several ways of looking at it," answered Sam, pinching the ends off a thin cigarette and lighting it. "It could lead us to a dead-end, for one thing. It could take us to a flash job and a business of our own. Or it could lead us into a whole swag of trouble. It could lead us into the sea or into those mountains up there. It could lead us into the grave—

anywhere. Y'see, Ponto old boy, it's not the road itself but the way you travel it. Some blokes bowl straight past some of the best things that are ever likely to happen to them because they don't see them. They're too busy looking towards the end of the journey to get a kick out of the travelling."

Ponto wasn't impressed. "It's all very well to talk about what might happen but I'd sooner have a good feed under my belt than all the talk in the world. A man can get by without talk but he can't go without a feed for long."

"That's just where you're wrong," said Sam. "The way things are today there's more money made with talk than hard work. Take any job you like; who gets the most money, the bloke who does the work or the one that gives the orders?"

He threw Ponto his coat and led the way on to the road.

They strolled along the winding, dipping, bushlined, stony road at a leisurely couple of miles an hour, which Ponto complained was a mad dash to get nowhere on an empty stomach. They were alternately in sunshine and shadow because of the semi-summer clouds that were breathing across the sun on a light west wind.

Sam was telling Ponto a yarn to keep his mind off his stomach.

"Talk about a liar! He was one out of the box, this bloke. One of them blokes who couldn't tell the truth if you paid him to. Must have been knocked around a bit when he was a kid or something. If you happened to mention something about fishing he'd tell you how he used to ride the tiger-sharks around in the sea off the Barrier Reef for a bit of sport. If anyone started talking about horses he'd chip in with a yarn about sneaking up on a brumby stallion in the dark, leaping on its back and riding it into town fully broken-in, with a few extra tricks thrown in, by daylight.

"If you said something about cows this bloke'd dig up a yarn about how he kept a mad Jersey bull from doing any more damage by playing it round the paddock like a dirty big trout, using his oilskin for a matador's cape, until the army got there and killed it with anti-tank guns!"

At this point Ponto snorted disgustedly but couldn't help grinning a little.

"He told me once," continued Sam, "that he used to creep up and hypnotise South American cougars and sell them to the zoos for thirty quid a throw. Once, he reckoned, when he was giving them a hand to load one on to a ship, the cage slipped out of the sling and busted. The cougar got loose and galloped up the main street of Brazil with Shai—that's this bloke's name—flat out after it. He grabbed it just as it was climbing in the window of the Lord Mayor's bedroom and slapped a full-nelson on it and carted it back to the wharf. But he put a bit too much pressure on and broke its neck. Done his thirty quid cold, but he got a medal off the government for bravery. He'd lost the medal in a two-up game a couple of weeks before so he couldn't show it to us.

"Then there was the time this coot reckoned he was logging down south somewhere in the middle of winter. The snow was so deep they used to wander through a block of bush, cutting the heads off the trees so they had all good clean logs to fell when the snow thawed. It was so cold the smoke used to freeze as soon as it left the chimney and roll down the roof and pile up in heaps round the hut. They had to spend a couple of hours every day rolling these big hunks of smoke away from the hut and piling them up in a gully behind the camp. When the thaw came they were smoke-bound in the hut for nearly a week. One of the blokes went out to the woodblock for an armful of wood and wandered around in the smoke for two days trying to find his way back to the hut. When the smoke cleared they organised a search party and found him nearly dead from exposure about fifty yards away from the hut. He was as black as the inside of a chimney from all the smoke. They warmed him up and scraped him down, but he died of lung cancer about six months later."

Sam paused and shook his head. "Yep, she must have been

cold all right. Even in the summer he reckoned she was always well below zero. One night there they were snigging a dirty big log out just before dark when she broke off and rolled into a little creek so they left it there till next day. When they went to drag it out in the morning she was frozen solid. Even the D-9 couldn't shift her so they got another tractor on to it.

"They pushed and pulled and bladed and ploughed for about three hours but the log stayed frozen into the creek as solid as ever. When they gave up and knocked off for lunch somebody suddenly noticed that they'd dragged the creek two hundred yards off-course."

Sam glanced at Ponto shuffling along beside him. "How's that for a beaut, Ponto?"

"I'm still bloody hungry," said Ponto ungraciously.

"Then this joker said how the Alaskan Government got to hear how good he was with animals and sent for him to go up there and deal with a pack of timber-wolves that were cleaning up all the Eskimo kids on their way home from school. He flew up to the Yukon with a big bag of macaroni and killed off thirty-eight timber-wolves without firing a single shot.

"He hollowed out lumps of meat, filled them with macaroni and dropped them from a helicopter. The wolves ate the meat and the macaroni swelled up inside them till they couldn't move. Then he landed and went round and finished them off with a young bull-terrier bitch he had in the back of the helicopter. He reckoned he could have done a better job using rice but macaroni was easier to get hold of at the time.

"That night he had a few beers with Dangerous Dan McGrew and flew back to Napier. That's where I ran into him. He was heading down to Wellington to see Wally Nash about a job. Very hush-hush, he reckoned it was. All he could say about it was that a big crack was opening up under one of the caissons on the Auckland Harbour Bridge and he was the only one who could save the whole thing from collapsing.

"He stung my mate for a couple of quid because they

wouldn't cash his Alaskan cheque at the bottle-store and he'd had to post it up to the Alaskan Embassy in Auckland. He didn't have time to wire his accountant for funds because he'd taken out a contract with the Yale University to supply them with poisonous snakes next year and it only left him three weeks to fix up the bridge and get over to America.

"My mate reckoned that Shai was the best value he'd had for two quid in all his life."

"Serves him right," said Ponto. "If he's dumb enough to believe a bloody joker who reckons smoke freezes he deserves to lose his two quid. He wouldn't get two bob out of me, I can tell you."

"Me mate reckoned it was worth it," said Sam. "Y'see, he was so wrapped up in listening to Shai that he forgot to go and meet his girl friend. He turned up an hour late, still grinning about Shai. His girl was pretty worked up by this time and what with my mate grinning and scoffing to himself she ups and breaks off the engagement. My mate was tickled pink. He came straight back to the pub and offered Shai another two quid. But Shai said the first two was enough to see him right. Just goes to show. A man never knows what way his luck's going to go from one minute to the next."

"I'm still bloody hungry," was Ponto's only comment.

"Hungry!" said Sam. "Hungry! Now *you're* exaggerating!"

Dan's Yarn

"Strike, Sam. Look at that big fat joker in the lead there!"

"Not so loud," whispered Sam urgently. "And get down. If they spot us we've had it."

Ponto settled back into the hedge and cleared a little opening in the long grass so he could look out.

"They're angling up the hill," said Sam. "They'll probably strike this hedge a bit further along. Keep an eye on them and if they head this way get ready to sneak back over the hill towards the road."

"How long will we have to wait?" asked Ponto.

"It'll be properly dark in about half an hour. We'd better give them about ten or fifteen minutes after that to settle down."

"Are you sure we can manage with only that sheet of corrugated iron?"

"Course we can. You can bake bread on a sheet of iron if you go the right way about it. We'll just cut the meat into strips and lay it on the tin on top of a fire."

"They're going into the hedge," said Ponto excitedly.

"Good," said Sam peering out past Ponto. "Mark the spot where they go in. We don't want to kick up too much of a racket thrashing around looking for them in the dark."

"They're right opposite that forked stump there."

"Good. They must be in good nick. When they bed down this early you can be pretty sure they're well-fed. I'll just keep an eye out on the other side of the hedge to make sure they don't go right through."

"Good idea. I'll watch this side in case they come out again."

"Ever swiped turkeys before?" asked Sam.

"Yeah, dozens of times. Nearly got caught once or twice too."

"You've got to be careful," said Sam. "They're pretty hot on swiping turkeys and stuff these days. I remember once when an old bloke called Dan and I were on a fowl-raid in a shed behind a cocky's house. We had about four each and just as we were sneaking out Dan goes and knocks a perch down with about thirty fowls on it. You'd think it was New Year's Eve. Fair go! There was flapping and squawking and dogs barking and lights going on and Dan and I standing in the yard with big handfuls of luminous white chooks. Then someone started yelling out from the house and a big bloke, about six foot four and tare somewhere round two hundred pounds, came out on to the back porch with an old army rifle."

"You'd have a job talking your way out of that one," grinned Ponto. "How did you get away?"

"Bloody quickly, I can tell you," said Sam. "I went one way and Dan stayed where he was. The bloke saw me dash through the yard and took off after me, firing shots in the air. As soon as we were clear Dan ducked back past the house and a woman started screaming her head off. The bloke left off chasing me and went rushing back yelling, 'Where? Where?'

"I sneaked back to pick up a couple of chooks I'd dropped and heard a terrible crash and then shouting and thumping and cursing. I thought Dan must have run fair into this bloke's arms. It wasn't till next day I found out what happened."

Sam began rolling a smoke and peered out of the hedge.

"Getting dark," he said. "We'll be able to get crackin' shortly."

"Well?" said Ponto.

"Well what?"

"What the hell had happened?"

"Happened to who?" asked Sam innocently.

"Happened to this bloke Dan with all the yelling and going on?" demanded Ponto impatiently.

"Oh, that! Well the day after, I was going past Dan's place

and here he is sitting on the front porch all battered and beaten around with.

"When the bloke heard his wife screaming and went back to see what was going on, he spotted Dan and made a rush at him. Dan jumped a fence and took to his scrapers. He'd just got himself into top gear when a clothes-line caught him fair under the chin. Just about tore the poor sod's head off. He must have done about half a dozen back somersaults. Lost all his chooks. The bloke came charging up shouting, 'I've got 'im! I've got 'im!' Dan dived out of the way just as the bloke pounced on him but he got his clod-hoppers hooked up in the clothes-prop and came another gutser. Dan reckons the bloke was just about frothing at the mouth by this time and roaring like a mad bull. Dan grabbed the clothes-prop and held the bloke off while he got on to his feet. Then he threw the prop and lit out for the road. He only got about fifty yards and went fair into a dirty big drain, full of blackberry and up to his guts in water. The bloke heard him fall in and came charging up with the clothes-prop and started slashing and belting and poking among the blackberry with it.

"He didn't find Dan but it was nearly daylight by the time Dan got home. I gave the poor sod one of my chooks so he wouldn't lose too much faith in things."

"He was a bit stiff on it all right," said Ponto. "His luck must have gone crook on him."

"It did that time," agreed Sam. "But Dan was always running into trouble like that and most of the time it was his own fault. He'd never stop to nut things out properly. He got had up once for swiping a Muscovy duck because he didn't even wait till it got properly dark before he started work on the duck-run gate.

"Ten days later he was in court. By that time the charges included the attempted theft of all the ducks—I don't know how he was supposed to carry them—damage to the gate and fence, breaking five panes of a glasshouse and twenty pots with plants in, upsetting a bird bath, turning a herd of cows loose and pinching a little kid's bike. He'd pedalled about a mile before they caught him and Dan reckoned he'd have made it if the back wheel of the bike hadn't buckled on him. He went back for the duck later, just to show he wasn't sore or anything.

"Dan had a big family and he was always on the lookout for a bit of cheap tucker to feed them on," continued Sam. "I remember once Dan and I were sinking a few pots in the local boozer and Dan started wondering what they used to do for meat before bows and arrows were invented. I told him I'd heard somewhere how a crowd of those cave-men blokes used to round up a mob of wild horses or cattle and get them stampeding flat-out towards a bluff. There was always one or two that couldn't pull up in time. They'd fall over and get killed and the cave-blokes could climb down and get them.

"Strike me pink, Ponto, within a week the odd yearling Hereford was falling over a big bluff on a sheep-station near Dan's place; and every time Dan just happened to be passing by. He'd give the skin to the owner and take the meat home for his dogs. And Dan never had a dog to bless himself with. Then he got a contract to fence off the top of the bluff, but he took his time over it."

"He wouldn't get away with it for long," said Ponto. "They'd wake up to that one pretty smartly."

"Yep, Dan gave himself away in the finish," said Sam. "He bowls up to the boss one day and tells him another yearling's gone over the bluff and can he have the meat for dog-tucker. Then the boss says he thinks he'll come out and have a look at where all these cattle have been falling over. Dan tells him not to bother, but the boss says he thinks he'll come all the same. They went out in the boss's Landrover and got there just in time to see two of Dan's boys chase a nice fat little heifer over the top."

"Did they put him up?" asked Ponto.

"No, they didn't put him up," replied Sam. "But Dan did a lot of free fencing for that bloke. Took him about six months to work off the price of the cattle he'd knocked off."

"Well, you can't say he didn't ask for it," said Ponto. "He was lucky to get away so light."

"On the other hand he was unlucky not to get away scot-free," said Sam. "I can't help thinking he could have still been getting a bit of free meat now and again if he'd handled it right. As I said, Dan never would stop to nut things out for himself . . . but it's just about time to make a move. We'll creep slowly up on them. Keep well in under the hedge and don't make any noise or we'll go hungry."

"Would you like me to wait here?" said Ponto nervously. "Two of us might scare them."

"No, you'd better come with me. That way you can keep a better lookout for anyone coming."

Sam led the way on his hands and knees along the hedge. They were about halfway to where the turkeys had settled for the night when Ponto tugged at Sam's foot and hissed: "Hey, there's a bloke up there!"

"Where—oh yes, I can see the bastard."

"He's sneaking up on us. Let's get out of here."

"No. Hang on a minute . . . ah, I thought so. He's after the turkeys. We'll just wait here and see what happens."

"Let's get out of it," insisted Ponto. "He's a big joker."

"He's only a kid," corrected Sam. "We'll let him grab a bird and then take it off him. He's going into the hedge now."

There was a bit of rustling and gobbling and flapping from up ahead and the young bloke came out of the hedge and began to walk away. Sam got up and hurried after him. Ponto hung back.

"Hang on there son," said Sam coming up behind the boy. "What do you think you're up to?"

The young bloke got a hell of a fright. The turkey nearly got away from him.

"What do you mean?" he stammered.

"Where do you think you're going with that turkey?"

"Home," said the boy. Sam saw that he was only about fourteen years old.

"I think you'd better give me the turkey," said Sam, "and cut along home. If I catch you up here again I'll be down to see your father." He reached for the turkey but the boy clutched it a bit harder and said: "But they're my father's turkeys. I've been sent up to get one for tomorrow—it's Friday."

Sam did a bit of quick thinking. This was a bit awkward.

"Where do you live?" he asked.

"In the house just over the hill there," said the boy pointing.

It was rarely that Sam couldn't think of anything to say. The boy was obviously telling the truth.

Suddenly from along the hedge came tremendous flapping and thrashing, and turkeys flew out of the trees in all directions. Then Ponto backed out holding a struggling turkey by one foot. Sam could just make out his stocky shambling figure as it lumbered off towards the road with all the subtlety of a runaway bulldozer, leaving a trail of noise and feathers half a chain wide behind him.

"What's that?" cried the young bloke.

Sam saw that the boy was thoroughly frightened. "That must be the man I saw sneaking up on your father's turkeys," he said sternly. "I'd better get after him. Tell your father I'll be round to see him later. There's got to be a stop put to all this thievery."

And he hurried off after Ponto, catching him down by the road clutching the turkey as though it was going to melt.

"What the hell did you want to go and do that for?" he asked.

"I was bloody hungry," said Ponto.

"Why didn't you wait a bit? I just about had the young bloke talked into thinking we went up there to save his old man's turkeys when you go and flog one and scatter the rest all over the farm. What was all the racket for anyway?"

"The one I wanted got away from me," said Ponto, "so I made a grab at the nearest one I could see and this was it . . . bit skinny but we'll get a feed off him," he added, poking hopefully at the boniest old ewe-turkey Sam had ever seen.

It was so quiet you could almost hear the sandflies coming. Ponto hobbled stiffly across to where Sam stood in the doorway thinking.

"What's it look like?" he asked.

"She's going to rain like hell before we get half a mile," said Sam without turning.

"Then we'd better stay where we are till it clears up."

"Yeah—or until we get caught in here," agreed Sam.

"Good, I'm going back to bed," said Ponto. And he did.

Sam stayed where he was, looking across the hills beyond the road. He was still leaning there when the rain swept across the paddocks and burst against the corrugated iron of the woolshed as suddenly as bullets. He slid the door shut and went across to Ponto's bunk.

"We're only a few miles out of Murchison," he said, leaning against the wool-press and getting Ponto's tobacco out of his coat-pocket. "Shouldn't take us long to get there, once it clears up."

The pile of sacks and sheepskins stirred a little. "What?"

"Do you think this brother of yours would come and pick us up if we got him on the phone?" asked Sam.

Ponto became very sleepy all of a sudden. He stirred some more, grunted a couple of times and mumbled, "Not on the phone."

"Could we get one of the neighbours to take a message to him, then?"

"Don't think it'd be any use," murmured Ponto, "he hasn't got a car."

"Doesn't sound as though it'd do us any harm to give this brother of yours a miss," said Sam casually.

The heap became agitated as Ponto sat up.

"Y'know," he said, standing up without even being stiff at the knees, "that's just what I was thinking! If we just happen to miss out with brother Bert there'll be no other job for miles!"

"We can't afford to risk that," said Sam solemnly, turning away with a faint grin. "We'd better stick to the main road."

Four Pounds Ten

"Three quid and a few loose bob—might just give us three-ten altogether." Ponto put the notes carefully back in his coat-pocket.

"And I've got a quid left out of the fiver I borrowed off you," said Sam.

"We'll have to give up eating flash tucker," said Ponto, as though that was the solution to his growing fear that one day soon he was going to have to cut more scrub, or take on some other kind of work.

"Might pay us to keep an eye open for a job," said Sam. "Our money isn't going to last more than another three or four days at the most."

"Too right!" enthused Ponto unenthusiastically. "It's about time a man got cracking on a bit of solid work again. I'll be getting soft on it! Haven't done a stroke since I slogged me guts out on that big contract up in the Sounds."

"We'll get hold of a paper and see what's advertised," said Sam. "It won't take us long to get an idea what's going on round the place."

"Yeah," said Ponto, slightly staggered at the suddenness of the way Sam did things. "You thinking of taking out a scrub-contract?"

"The only time you'd ever catch me cutting scrub was if it was in my road," said Sam. "And I'm not going out of my way to put any there."

This sounded better to Ponto. "That's exactly what I think," he said quickly. "I only suggested it because I thought you might like to have a try at it. Wouldn't have mentioned it otherwise."

"When you've cut as much scrub as I have, Ponto me lad," said Sam standing up and patting him on the shoulder, "you won't even suggest it. Let's go and get that paper."

"Where the hell are we anyway?" asked Ponto.

Sam uncurled himself from the seat and moved stiffly to the door of the railway carriage. They'd slept in worse places but it was time to get moving. He looked up and down the tracks to see if anyone was watching. "Longfield," he read from the end of the goods-shed along the line. "Come on, there's nobody around."

They crossed the tracks and climbed through the fence on to the road. There was a pub, a garage, a store, a tea-rooms, and the railway station scattered along two hundred yards of the main road and called Longfield. Ponto veered off towards the pub but Sam guided him expertly back in the direction of the tea-rooms.

They had scrambled eggs on toast for breakfast because that was all they could get; and yesterday's paper because today's hadn't arrived yet. Ponto's attitude towards his page of the Situations Vacant section suggested that last year's paper would have been better.

"Nothing much doing in here," announced Sam putting aside his page. "What's yours look like, Ponto?"

"Not a thing, nothing at all," said Ponto quickly, folding his paper and putting it out of sight on a spare seat beside him.

"I see there's plenty of jobs going in Christchurch," said Sam. "It's not very far from here. Looks like we'll have to go there and see what we can get on to. Contract work—or any kind of work in the country—isn't going to be much good to us. It never stops raining round here this time of year."

"You been here before, Sam?"

"Yeah," said Sam in a way that didn't inspire Ponto to ask any more about it.

"Got a sister in Christchurch," said Ponto a little later, when they were on the road waiting for a lift. "Married to a Dutch bloke. Pots of dough, rolling in the stuff. We could tap her for a few quid easy enough."

"We probably could," said Sam with a look at an empty car that sneered past them with an averted face at the wheel. "But we can't make a living out of tapping people for money all the time or I'd have been at it for years. The only way to make a quid that's really yours is to get it off someone who does all the worrying about where it comes from and where it goes to. And the only way to do that is to work for it at a job you can leave behind when you go home at night. A man gets old quick enough without worrying his head over other people's money having to be paid back. And as far as money goes, the better off a man is the worse off he is in other ways. It's not good for people to have too much of the stuff. They're so busy looking after it that they haven't got time to be people."

"I s'pose you're right," admitted Ponto, "but I wouldn't mind having a few thousand quid in the old kick, all the same."

"Why?"

"Oh, I don't know, Sam. Makes a man feel more confident somehow."

"Fair enough, but what do you reckon you'd do if you had enough loot so you didn't ever have to work again?"

"I'd throw a big party for the first bloke who gives us a lift," said Ponto. "I think it's going to start raining again."

"I'll tell you what you'd do," said Sam with an unnecessary glance at the sky. "You'd drink yourself to death so fast you wouldn't have a chance to get a taste of the stuff."

"And what do you reckon you'd do?" asked Ponto, obviously not at all disturbed at the idea of pulling the chain on himself in such a pleasant way.

"Me?" Sam paused, squinting at nothing in the middle distance. "I'd keep a quid for myself and give the rest to people who were hard up and needed operations on their eyes and lungs and things. Then I'd go on wearing out my boots and my brains keeping dozy coots like you out of trouble."

Ponto, giving way at last to a curiosity that had been nagging at him ever since that night in Picton, suddenly asked: "What have you been doing mostly all your life, Sam?—I mean, where do you come from and that?"

Sam gave him a subject-changing look and said, "Just knocking around," in a subject-changing voice.

They didn't say anything else that mattered for about half an hour, until a truckload of bitter-tasting apples stopped and gave them a lift right into Christchurch. There was plenty of time to look through the paper for jobs, which Ponto thought was sprung on him so suddenly as to be quite unfair, but he had nothing to worry about. They whittled four pages of Situations Vacant down to the four jobs that offered accommodation, took two of these each, and set off with apparent enthusiasm to find work—"just enough to keep us moving", as Ponto said.

Sam turned down work on a drainage project that offered insufficient money for an eight-hour day in two feet of mud, and ignored the bait of an old swindler who wanted land cleared for housing and thought he could get mugs cheaper than machines.

Ponto set off half an hour early towards where he was to meet Sam but on the way he got lost and arrived nearly half an hour late with such a weak-sounding hard-luck yarn that Sam almost believed he'd actually been and asked about the jobs. They headed for a good pub Ponto had found where they could talk things over "with a glass of suds in our mitts".

"The only thing to do," said Sam, "is to clear out of here and the only way to do it is to gather a few quid so we can. And the only way to gather a few quid is for you to go and get a job."

"Here, what about you getting a bloody job?"

"Don't worry, Ponto old boy. You'll get the job and I'll make the money. All you have to do is one day's work."

"I don't like the sound of it," said Ponto. "What are you going to do?"

"The less you know about it the better it'll work. Just take my word for it. I've never let you down yet, have I? Just you leave it to Uncle Sam."

Sam booked Ponto into a private hotel and then visited him "to discuss business" in the evening. Ponto had to be almost man-handled into the bath after Sam had finished with it. The razor Sam found in the bathroom cabinet only had one blade and by the time Ponto started using it the thing was painfully blunt. But they managed. They put their trousers under the mattress to be ironed and it was the first real bed they'd slept in for several days, though it was a little on the narrow side for Ponto and the short side for Sam.

Sam got away early in the morning to avoid upsetting the landlady and met Ponto on a nearby corner after breakfast. They looked almost respectable in their clean-shaven faces and pressed trousers. Sam dropped a couple of little stones into an honesty-box and took a morning paper, explaining that he once put two bob in a box in Auckland and still had a credit of one and ninepence.

Sam read out an advertisement for a driver's assistant and generously told Ponto he could have a go at landing it. Ponto took the address and went around the nearest corner to waste time. They arranged to meet outside the hotel at one o'clock.

Sam strolled away in the opposite direction.

Ponto wandered along looking in shop windows and wondering what to do. He threw his screwed-up piece of newspaper in the gutter and bought himself a pie. Then he sat on a bench at a bus-stop and watched the people going past. After that he waited for half an hour in a public lavatory.

Sam went into a pub.

"Beer?" asked the barman.

"Yeah, give us an eight," said Sam digging in his pocket.

He was still searching his pockets when the barman had finished pouring the beer.

"I'll have to duck out to the car," he said, reaching for the glass. "I've left me wallet in the glove-box. Fill 'er up again while I'm gone, will you?"

But the barman grabbed the beer first. "You can have this when you get back," he said.

"Okay," said Sam carelessly. "Suit yourself."

He sauntered out singing the wrong words of "Home on the Range" to the wrong tune and found another pub, where he paid for his beer.

Ponto was strolling up and down a back street. On his second trip past, he stopped across the road from a big sign saying: LABOURERS WANTED. APPLY WITHIN. He crossed to have a closer look at what kind of a place it was and peered through a doorway into a big dim shed that turned out to be a cabinet-making factory.

A few men were hammering and screwing and stacking and fitting at long benches, and machines hummed and buzzed at the far end of the building. The place stank of sawdust, glue and hard work. Ponto didn't hear the bloke come up the footpath behind him until a voice at his shoulder said: "Can I help you, sir?"

Ponto started violently. "I was just looking at the sign there," he said, completely off his guard.

"Yes, we need men. Come on in and I'll show you what we do here."

"Well actually I've never had any experience at this kind of thing," stammered Ponto. "Never was much good at woodwork."

"That's all right," said the man pleasantly, leading Ponto into the building by the elbow. "We can put you on a machine that doesn't require any special knowledge or experience."

"Oh I couldn't handle a machine," said Ponto. "They make me nervous."

"Well, we can always use a man on the old glue-pot," said the man understandingly. "The pay's just the same. There's a quiet little corner over here . . ."

It was half an hour before Ponto could get away, saying he'd ring up and let the bloke know.

At half-past twelve Sam was strolling back to meet Ponto when he caught sight of him on the corner up ahead, peering round into the street where they were to meet. Evidently Ponto didn't intend getting there first.

Sam backed away and doubled round to find a corner of his own. On his way he called in at a greengrocer's shop and complained that a lettuce his wife had bought there yesterday was rotten in the centre—just to keep his hand in. The little Chinaman shuffled out to the back of the shop and brought another little Chinaman back with him, who informed Sam that they hadn't had a lettuce in the place for over three weeks.

"Must be the wrong shop," said Sam casually, tossing a Granny Smith up and down in front of the Chinamen a few times and then going out.

He finished his apple and circled round to the meeting-place. Ponto arrived shortly afterwards

"How did you get on, Ponto?"

"No good. I tried everywhere. If the job's any good the pay's crook. Things are tough around here, I tell you."

"No one offered you a job at all?"

"Well I managed to talk one bloke into offering me one, but it's a lousy sort of a set-up. Woodwork factory—glueing stuff."

"Sounds easy enough. What did you tell them?"

"Said I'd ring up and let them know but they'll know I don't want the job when I don't turn up."

"You'll have to take it," said Sam. "It's only for one day and it's the only way we can get away from here. What are they paying?"

Ponto was looking as though he'd just been reminded of an old gambling debt.

"Now look, Sam," he said, "we don't want to go rushing madly into the first job that gets thrown at us. Let's just wait a while and see if anything better turns up."

"No go, Ponto old boy. For what we want, one job's as good as another. You don't want to be stuck in a place like this with no money, do you? How much an hour did they say it was worth?"

"Six and six an hour," muttered Ponto sullenly. "Bloke said it worked out at about thirteen quid a week clear—with bloody overtime."

Ponto arrived at work half an hour late the next morning, looking hostile and trapped and not quite sure what was going to happen. He'd had jobs before, hundreds of them, and he didn't like the look of this one any more than he had the others. As he walked into the factory the foreman hurried over to meet him.

"You're late," he said, looking at his watch. "When you phoned I told you . . ."

"I know that," said Ponto. He couldn't keep the trace of a snarl out of his voice.

The foreman looked at him for a few moments before saying: "Well if you'll just come in here I'll get you to fill out your tax form and then get you started."

Half an hour later Ponto was standing at a bench with a big pot of glue, sticking handles into children's rattles and passing them to another bloke who was testing them and packing them into boxes. Above the bench was a sign saying: IT IS ESSENTIAL TO ALLOW THE ELAPSE OF SUFFICIENT TIME FOR THE MIGRATION OF THE SOLVENTS FROM THE JUXTAPOSED INTERFACES OF THE WORK BEING GLUED.

"What's that supposed to mean?" he asked the bloke next to him.

The bloke glanced at the sign and said: "It means to stop

splashing that bloody glue all over the place and don't go so fast, I can't keep up."

But by lunchtime the bench, the floor, the rattles, the boxes and Ponto were covered with glue, and the bloke next to him had a big pile of sticky rattles to test and pack.

After lunch the other bloke took over the glueing and Ponto the testing and packing. The foreman came over to see how they were getting on and the other bloke got ticked off for wasting glue and Ponto was told to keep the bench clear.

Sam was in a pub with their last thirty bob and a bloke he'd made friends with, a wharfie who was "on compo" with a sprained thumb.

"You just wouldn't believe it, Bob," Sam was saying. "The laziest coot you've ever seen in your life. One of them blokes who goes around looking as though he's just woken up in the middle of a hot afternoon all the time. I think he wants watching too. I haven't quite got him sorted out yet but he'll turn out to be a ratbag as sure as I'm riding this bike."

Bob put his empty glass on the bar beside Sam's and said: "He sounds a bit of a crook one all right. What do you want to hang around with him for? Drop him off and come down and work on the wharf with us. I can get you a job there, no trouble."

"Thanks all the same, Bob," said Sam gratefully. "But a man doesn't want to desert a mate just because he's no good—besides, I want to find out what makes this bloke tick. There's something queer about him and I want to know what it is. You never know, a bit of work might just bring him right. If he can stick this job out for a week I might change my mind about him, but I can't see him lasting more than a couple of days at the most."

"He must be chronic," said Bob. "You've got more patience than I have, Sam. I wouldn't put up with a shiftless coot like that for five minutes."

"I don't mind him bludging on my hard work so much," said Sam generously, "but I can't stand a man who'd put one across his mates."

"What, has he done you down, Sam?"

"Well, I'd rather not discuss it, Bob, if you don't mind. If I can't say anything good about a bloke I'd sooner keep my mouth shut."

Sam managed a magnificent martyred look and Bob shook his head sadly in sympathy.

"I know how it is, Sam. If you take my advice you'll make a break as soon as you can."

"I don't know, Bob. I guess I'm just not that kind of a joker. Couldn't run out on a bloke to save myself. I'm not made that way. I'll just go on knocking around with him and hope for the best."

Bob shouted the drinks for the third time in a row. "I used to do a fair bit of knocking around myself," he said, "but not these days. Getting married knocks that off."

"You a married man, Bob?"

"Yep. Eight years of it. Wouldn't swap it for anything either. —Hell, that reminds me. I've got to get a blasted birthday present for one of the kids."

"How old?"

"Seven, my oldest boy. Got another one, five."

"There's only one thing to get a lad that age for his birthday," said Sam philosophically.

"What's that?" asked Bob interestedly. "I was thinking of getting him a toy truck or something."

"Nar," said Sam, sliding his empty glass across the bar. "Get him something like that and what happens?—It either gets swiped or busted within a few days. And why? I'll tell you why—because the young bloke loses interest in it and doesn't look after it properly, and your money's gone down the drain."

"Yeah, I know," said Bob. "You're dead right, but what else is there? Everything goes the same way."

"Get him a dog," said Sam decisively. "You can't go wrong."

"A dog?" Bob was sceptical.

"Yep. A dog. It doesn't even matter what kind of a dog it is. Take home a dog and I'll guarantee the young feller thinks all his birthdays have come at once!"

"I wouldn't know where to look for one," said Bob. "Besides . . ."

"Hang on," interrupted Sam. "Now who was it who was asking me just the other day . . . Ah, I've got it—Harvey Wilson! I think I might just be able to help you out here, Bob. A mate of mine wants to get rid of a pup. Been a kid's pet all its life. They don't want to part with it but they're going overseas and have to find a good home for it. I'll probably be able to get it cheap for you if it hasn't already gone."

"I don't think I'll bother with it, thanks all the same, Sam. I'd have to ask the missus in any case."

"No, you don't want to do that, Bob. Give 'em a surprise! Ever know the wife to go crook when you bring home something unexpected?"

"You don't know my old woman," said Bob.

"Okay. Tell you what I'll do with you. I'll see if I can get the dog for you and if your missus goes hostile about it I'll take it myself. You can't lose. I'll ring this bloke right now and see if the dog's still available."

Without waiting for Bob to comment on this idea Sam went into the bottle-store, looked up an address and pretended to ring up. Then he hurried back to the bar and said excitedly to Bob: "I think we're just in time. Wait here. I'll be back in a few minutes."

He dashed out and got himself a taxi.

"Take me to the S.P.C.A.," he said to the driver.

Sam came back into the pub leading a scruffy old spaniel bitch with a stiff hind leg, and passed Bob the rope with a pleased grin.

"There y'are, Bob," he said proudly. "How's that!"

"Look, it's pretty good of you, Sam," said Bob, eyeing the

dog. "But I don't think the missus'd be too keen on it."

"Well if she doesn't like it bring it back tomorrow and I'll take it off your hands," said Sam. "But I'll bet she's tickled pink about it, all the same." He lowered his voice and gave Bob a sly wink. "Knocked him down from five quid to four pound ten for you."

"It's got a stiff leg," said Bob.

"That's nothing," said Sam. "She got kicked by a horse when she was a pup. It doesn't make any difference though. She's very lively once she gets to know you."

"I thought you were going to get a pup?" said Bob desperately.

"That's where you're getting such a good bargain," said Sam blandly. "I got you this good breeding-bitch. You can get all the pups you want for nothing."

So Bob got a crippled, shivering wreck of a dog he didn't particularly want and Sam got four pounds ten he did want.

Men at Work

When he met Ponto for a drink after work Sam was in a jovial mood. He patted Ponto on the back and told him how much healthier he was looking after doing an honest day's work. Ponto muttered savagely and drank Sam's beer for him.

Ponto smelled strongly of the glue and sawdust that was streaked all over his clothes, and Sam said it might be a good idea to get cleaned up a bit, in case he got run in for scaring kids or something.

"You remind me of a pup that's been rolling in something," he joked. "We'll have to shout you a pinny if you don't improve by the end of the week."

But Ponto wasn't going to be cheered up. "How much longer do I have to go on working in that dump?" he said sullenly.

"We'll give 'er a couple of hours in the morning and then spring it on them," said Sam.

"It's all very well for you," complained Ponto, reaching again for Sam's beer, "but I'm the one who has to do all the bloody work."

"Work!" cried Sam indignantly. "Work! I've been flat-out to it all day. Haven't had a moment's rest—look at this!" And he flashed a handful of four one-pound notes as though it was a great roll of fivers.

"Struth, Sam! Where did you get all that?"

"I'm working a little deal," said Sam mysteriously, looking up and down the bar to see if anyone was listening. "Can't talk about it in here," he whispered, drawing Ponto a little closer. "Too risky. You never know who's listening in on a bloke."

"Hope you know what you're doing," said Ponto, much more cheerful than he had been. "Where did you get that money?"

Sam winked mysteriously and peeled off a pound for Ponto as though it was a tenner.

"That's for spending cash," he said expansively. "By the time we're finished here we'll be able to take our time looking round for a decent job."

Ponto went through the formality of putting the pound in his pocket and then placed it on the bar beside his empty glass.

Ponto was three-quarters of an hour late getting to work next morning. The foreman informed him that his pay would be docked and that he was to go on a different job today. Bagging up sawdust. Ponto took the shovel and the bags out to a big heap of sawdust behind the factory, filled one bag to just the right height and sat on it to roll himself a smoke. He felt a bit cheated that nobody noticed him loafing and gave him the sack.

Just after morning smoko the phone rang in the foreman's office.

"Atkin's Joinery," said the foreman lifting the receiver.

"Could I speak to Mr Downing please?" said a businesslike voice at the other end.

"Speaking. What can I do for you?"

"It's Harvey Wilson here, Mr Downing. I understand you've recently employed a man called Ponto Manson."

"Ah—yes, that's right."

"How is he getting along with the other chaps there?"

"Well, he only started yesterday. Why do you ask?"

"Perhaps I'd better explain. I'm with the Labour Department. Mr Manson has been causing us a good deal of bother lately. Nothing we can be absolutely certain about, you understand, but we've reason to believe he's been at the root of quite a bit of trouble in factories—getting at the other workers and causing discontent, and that kind of thing. Now we don't want to be hanging around the factory keeping an eye on him all the time. It would hardly be fair on you people, but as long as you keep a careful eye on him and let us know . . ."

"As a matter of fact," interrupted the foreman, "I'm not at all happy with this man's work, and if he's as bad as you say I think I'll get rid of him. There was a complaint yesterday and he'd only been on the job a couple of hours."

"Has he begun setting a bad example to the other chaps? You know, arriving late and that kind of thing?"

"Yes, he was half an hour late yesterday and nearly an hour late this morning."

"Yes, yes. I think in that case you'd be well advised to follow the course you suggest and get rid of him. It'd make it easier for us to keep him under observation at the same time. But for goodness sake don't give him any excuse to say he's been badly treated. He'll jump at the slightest chance to cause trouble and you don't want any more bother with him than you can help. Pay him for a full week and tell him that you've been forced to cut down on staff because of prices or something."

"Don't worry, Mr Wilson. I'll handle him carefully. I've had a bit of experience with these blokes. I knew there was something not quite right about this chap but I couldn't tell just what it was. I'm very grateful to you for having taken the trouble . . ."

"Think nothing of it, Mr Downing. Think nothing of it. Just doing our job, that's all. Now I won't take up any more of your valuable time. I know how busy you must be—Goodbye now."

"Goodbye, Mr Wilson. And thanks again."

"Thank *you*," said Sam, and hung up.

They were leaning on an otherwise deserted bar. The barman was trying not to listen. Ponto was doing most of the talking and rather more than half of the drinking.

"Yep," he boasted. "I told him, good and proper! He wanted

me to stay on, but I told him it was ten bob an hour or nothing. He wouldn't have that on. Most he'd raise it to was eight and six so I told him what to do with his bloody job. Then he offered to put me in charge of the spraying department, but I stuck to my guns. 'Give me my pay,' I says to him. And blow me down if he doesn't come clean with a whole week's pay. Just under twelve quid. Shows you how worried I had him, doesn't it!"

"Sure does," said Sam. "I didn't know you had it in you, Ponto."

"Oh I take a lot of getting aroused, but when I do—look out!"

"I'm a bit more inclined to go the quiet way, myself," said Sam. "I remember once when I was just a young bloke I was apprenticed to a cabinet-maker. Not a bad bloke really, but after a few weeks I got a bit fed up with the outfit. They had me sanding the rough edges off pieces of radio cabinet, day in and day out—you know the kind of thing."

"Sure do," said Ponto expertly.

"Well in the finish I bailed up the boss and told him I wasn't all that terribly keen on the idea of spending the rest of my life sanding rough edges off pieces of radio cabinet.

"So he put me on a saw-bench—cutting up bits of dowelling to make draughts with. I lasted about four days on that and then told the boss I didn't think I was cut out to be a draught-cutter-offer after all. So he put me on making thumb-holes in pencil-case lids. That one only lasted a day and a half. I told the boss I wasn't much of a thumb-hole-maker either. He told me to stick at it while he worked out another job for me, but he didn't seem to be in any hurry about it until I started accidentally putting the thumb-holes at the wrong end of the lids. He told me off for being careless so I stuck thumb-holes at both end of the lids, then in the middle. In the finish I was making little patterns of thumb-holes all over everything I could get my hands on.

"The boss was a little bit hot on that idea. He reckoned I

was bloody useless at making thumb-holes but I pointed out that they were getting pretty damn good with all the practice I was getting in. I think the boss got the idea I was having him on a bit because he put me on the worst job in the factory—assembling dolls' cots. The unlimited variety and scope for initiative the boss told me about when I started there came in handy on the doll-cot-assembly job. It was just like a dirty big Meccano set. I had some great fun till they caught me.

"We had a little pep-talk in the office.

" 'Aren't you happy here?' says the boss.

" 'No,' says I.

" 'Well, you'll have to take a pull on yourself,' says he. 'We can't have this sort of thing going on.'

" 'No,' says I.

" 'Well, Sammy,' he says, 'if there's any more of it I'll just have to think about replacing you, that's all there is to it.'

" 'I've got a better idea,' says I. 'Why don't you give me the bullet?'

"He thinks it over for a while and then says: 'No, Sammy. I don't want to do that. I'm sure you'll settle down here when you get used to the work.'

" 'I doubt it,' says I. 'I think I'll turn the job in.'

" 'You realise it's going to cost you fifty pounds to break your apprenticeship,' says he.

" 'Yeah,' says I. 'The only way we can work it is if you give me the sack.'

" 'Well I'm not going to,' says he, getting a bit nasty-looking on it. 'I'm putting you back on the sander and you can jolly well stay there!' "

Sam paused for a drink. The barman was listening openly by this time and Ponto was taking advantage of the distraction of Sam's yarn to switch his empty glass for Sam's full one every now and again.

"What happened after that?" asked the barman, forgetting for a moment that he wasn't in the game. "Did you go back on the sander?"

"Yes," said Sam, just beating Ponto to the draw on his fresh glass of beer. "I jolly well went back on his jolly old sander, but I didn't jolly well stay there too jolly long. All the jolly sander-belts started breaking on me. I was more than half the time fixing up new belts."

"So they had to sack you after all," said Ponto.

"Yeah," agreed Sam. "But not for that." He turned to the barman. "It's about time we had one on the house, isn't it?"

"Yeah. Sure, sure," said the barman grabbing the glasses.

"I was thinking of having a whisky this time," interrupted Ponto innocently.

"That's okay," said the barman. "Have it on me." He put Ponto's beer glass aside and reached for a whisky glass.

"As well as the beer," added Ponto.

The barman put the drinks on the bar and he and Ponto waited for Sam to continue.

"What *did* they sack you for?" asked Ponto after a few moments.

"Well at the time we'd been having a few power cuts. The sander was just underneath the main switchboard for the whole factory so I arranged a few little power cuts of my own. Just after smoko I'd reach up with a lump of wood and throw the master switch out of gear. All the machines would stop. The lights would go out and we'd all stand around waiting for the power to come on again. I'd arrange that for them just before lunch."

"How long before they caught you?" asked Ponto.

"Too long. It's funny about that. A bloke who doesn't care whether he gets caught can get away with blue murder and the bloke who works it crafty often gets copped straight off. It was nearly a week before the bloke who used to go out and buy the lunch for everybody noticed that we were the only ones who were having power cuts. All the other places were lit up and working. Of course he has to tell the boss all about it. Then somebody notices the main switch turned off and sets us up in business again. Then the boss comes over.

" 'Sammy,' he says. 'You're the nearest to the switchboard. Have you seen anybody interfering with it lately?'

" 'Do you mean have I seen anybody turning off the power?' says I.

" 'Yes,' says he.

" 'Yes,' says I.

" 'Well why didn't you report it?' says he.

" 'I don't like getting people into trouble,' says I.

" 'Who was it?' says he.

" 'I don't like telling tales,' says I.

" 'Now look, Sammy,' says he. 'You won't get into any trouble by just telling me who it was. I'll see to that. I won't even mention who told me.'

" 'Promise me there'll be no trouble?' says I.

" 'Sure, Sammy,' he says. 'I'm a man of my word, you know that.'

" 'Well in that case I don't mind telling you,' says I. 'It was me!' "

"Did that do the trick?" asked Ponto, putting Sam's empty glass back on the bar.

"The trick," said Sam. "It did half a dozen of them. The old boy just stood there gasping for a little while. You'd swear he was trying to swallow a handful of post staples or something. Then he did about four cartwheels, half a dozen handsprings, chinned himself a few times on his flash new overhead conveyor-belt and told me in a very quiet voice that I was sacked, as from that moment.

"I asked him for a reference but he didn't seem to think I deserved one. Miserable sort of a coot really. It wasn't till about two years later when they read the will of an old aunt of mine who died that I found out why he kept me on the job so long."

"What was the score on that one?" asked Ponto, sliding his glass expertly towards the barman.

"Well I was always a bit of a favourite with this aunt. She had more dough than she knew what to do with and I was the only one who wasn't scared to give the old girl a bit of lip now and again. All the other relatives were too busy thinking of the money to treat her like a human being, so I was the one she left all the loot to. And when they went through her gear they found where she'd slipped this wood bloke a few quid to make a decent sort of a cabinet-maker out of me. Thieving coot probably didn't want to lose out on the dough."

"How much did the aunt leave you, Sam?"

"Twenty-five thousand-odd quid," replied Sam nonchalantly, lighting a smoke.

"Strike me bloody pink," said Ponto. "And you've blown the lot!"

"No, I never got it," said Sam, sliding his beer out of Ponto's twitching reach.

"Why?"

"Well y'see, Ponto, there was a clause in the will that said I was to collect the money the day I finished my apprenticeship, and I never finished it."

"You're bloody mad!" said Ponto. "Twenty-five thousand quid for five years' work. You'll never get another chance to pick up money like that so easy."

"Nar," said Sam. "It'd be the toughest dough a man ever earned. You'd be better off working for your keep on a job you liked than loafing around getting big money for a job that bores you. Putting up with boredom is an easier habit to get into than out of. There's many a good man gone down the drain because he couldn't see past the money on a job he tackled. It's a matter of taking your pick between being rich or being a man, there's no compromise. Now let's get out of here while they've still got a bit of beer left for their regular customers."

"I still reckon you're bloody mad to let all that dough go," said Ponto, following Sam out into the street.

Hospitality

"It's too late to think of heading off anywhere today," said Sam. "We shouldn't have booked you out of that boarding-house. Now we'll have to see about a bunk for tonight."

"But we haven't booked me out of the boarding-house," said Ponto.

"Yes we have," said Sam.

"Oh," said Ponto. "In that case we'd better get clear of town before they report us."

"Don't panic," said Sam. "By the time the old girl livens that we're not coming back we'll be miles away."

"Well, where are we going to stay tonight?" said Ponto, looking with a shiver at the darkening sky.

"We'll think of something," said Sam. "We can't go squandering our hard-earned cash on paying hotel bills, that's for certain. You never get anywhere that way."

"Let's think it over in this pub," said Ponto, steering off towards a bar they were passing. "They run a thing called licensing hours round here."

"Okay," said Sam. "But go easy on the grog. We don't want to blow all our dough in pubs either."

It was after five o'clock and men were drinking three deep at the bar, but that didn't stop Ponto. He headed into them like a D-9 going downhill through fern and clamoured expertly for attention. Sam waited back against the wall where there was almost enough space to lift a drink. Ponto returned with four glasses of beer slopping in his hands.

"Got us a couple each," he explained superfluously. "Saves going back for more all the time."

By drinking three beers to Sam's one, Ponto had almost enough to drink by six o'clock. Sam timed his last drink so they just missed the bottle-store and Ponto's plan to "get a few bottles for the evening" fell through.

It was almost dark outside. They stood on the footpath getting in the way of people hurrying home to food and bed. A few layers of misty rain began to waft about in the wind. Ponto hummed loudly and tunelessly to himself. Sam was trying to work out how they could get on to a cheap bunk.

"I know!" said Ponto suddenly.

"What do you know?" said Sam.

"Where we can sleep—me sister Doris. We'll go and see her! She's a real good sort. Do anything for you."

"I'd forgotten you had a sister in Christchurch, Ponto," grinned Sam, amused at the prospect.

"My oath I have," said Ponto. "I know the address too. Let's grab a taxi and go out there. She'll probably want us to stay for a few days, but we'll get away somehow. Very hospitable."

Waiting at the taxi-rank Sam said to Ponto, "Your sister married, Ponto?"

"Yeah. To a Dutchman—but not a bad bloke, for all that. Keeps two jobs going and gets around on a little two-stroke motor-bike. Quiet sort of rooster. Hasn't got much to say for himself. You can't understand half what he's talking about anyway. He might be abusing a man half the time for all I know. He's a good worker," he added in an awestruck voice.

As they approached Doris's place Sam noticed that Ponto's beer seemed to be wearing off a little and that he knocked on the door a lot less confidently than his description of Doris's hospitality called for.

"Might be an idea not to say anything in front of her about us being on holiday most of the time," he whispered. "She's got some queer ideas about steady jobs and that."

The door was opened by a female Ponto. She looked as though she'd crack you one at the drop of a swear word, but turned out to be quite friendly.

"Hello, Peter," she said. "This *is* a surprise! Come on in—Who's your friend?"

"This is Sam . . . Me sister Doris."

"Pleased to meet you, Sam."

"G'day."

Doris looked as though she was going to shake hands with him for a moment but she changed her mind and let them into a kitchen so clean and shiny that Sam was stonkered for something to lean on.

"Take Sam through to the sitting-room, Peter. I'll bring you in a cup of tea in a moment. Jack's working night-shift at the new bakehouse now, you know. He gets more money than the last place but the hours are terrible. He doesn't get home until all hours. Still, his new boss is a nice chap. He never did get along with that awful Mr Collingwood. . . ."

Ponto, who'd recovered some of his cheek at the warmth of their reception, ushered Sam into the sitting-room and closed the door on his sister's description of Jack's last boss.

"Flash place, eh!" he said, waving around at the carpet and the china cabinet (loaded to the gunnels with useless and unused wedding presents) and the chairs and sofa and the gleaming piano with its crown of paper flowers, wax fruit and photographs.

Photographs! There were photos of Doris all over the place. Doris at weddings. Doris at dances and beaches and picnics. Doris shopping. Doris riding horses and bikes. Doris when she was a baby, a little girl, a medium-sized girl, a big girl, a choir girl, a marching-girl, a good girl, a good-time girl, etc., etc., etc.

"Yeah, it's flash all right," said Sam, making himself as at-home as possible in a chair as soft as a rich lady's rump, and getting out his tobacco. "Jack's a pretty unusual name for a Dutchman, isn't it, Ponto?" he asked.

"His real name sounds like Shark," explained Ponto loudly. "If you seen him you'd know why it had to be altered around a bit—poor coot."

Ponto's sister came in and Ponto continued: "Fine bloke Jack. One of the best. A real go-ahead type. Tackle anything. . . ."

"Pity you didn't arrive earlier, Peter," she said. "Jack and I had a special dinner for his birthday. Oysters and steak, finishing with apricot pie—it's all cold now, anyway. But you never fancied oysters, did you? Didn't seem to agree with you?"

"Oysters are all right," said Ponto, and Sam could see his mouth watering, "but I ate too many of them once when I was a kid." And on he went about "that time in Invercargill when oysters were so cheap that . . ."

Sam scowled inwardly as he realised that Doris had out-manoeuvred Ponto, as she had doubtless done many times in the past. The steak-and-onions smell was all they would get from her. He was wrong, but only just.

Doris gave them two ashtrays each, one cup of tea, three tiny biscuits and a solid hour of information on how to get through your housework by lunchtime each day (except Mondays because that was when she did the washing).

"Would you like me to take your coat, Sam?" said Doris in the middle of a sentence about Jack fixing his motor-bike on the front porch and getting oil on everything. "You must be roasting!"

"She'll be right, thanks," said Sam. "I feel the cold a fair bit, as a matter of fact."

Doris then fetched a big fan-heater and set it up in front of him.

"There now. That'll be more comfortable for you," she said, plugging it into a point beside his chair. "Some people do feel the cold a lot, I know. Jack likes to keep the room nice and warm when he's home."

Sam would have felt more at home in a courtroom. He squirmed uncomfortably in the blast of hot air from the heater and by the time Doris was properly under way with the motor-bike yarn again the sweat was prickling his scalp and draining down his neck and the sides of his face. He lasted out another ten minutes and then stood up. Doris stopped talking.

"Well Ponto, old boy. If we're going to meet that bloke we'd better step on it. He said he wouldn't wait for us if we were late."

"Yes, yes, that's right," said Ponto too quickly. "I didn't realise how late it was—Sorry we have to dash off, Doris."

"That's all right. You must call in again any time you're passing."

"Yes, we'll certainly do that," said Ponto enthusiastically, and he collected a look from Sam which said over Doris's shoulder: "Speak for yourself."

Doris kept them talking at the gate until Sam's sweat began to freeze.

They settled down for the night under a tarpaulin. "Guests of the Government", as Sam put it. It wasn't quite raining though the sky was in a bigger mess than two small, unattended boys could make of a living-room floor on a wet afternoon. The sounds and smells of the railway yards were brittle and clear in the chillness of the night air on their faces. Burnt and burning coal, a cattle-truck nearby, Ponto's breath, the crash and rumble of shunting.

Sam was watching the sky pour restlessly through a gap between two buildings and thinking about nothing in particular. Ponto was muttering blankly to himself about the way circumstances were treating him.

Sam suddenly chuckled, like a man who's just seen the joke.

"What's so funny?" grumbled Ponto, rustling uncomfortably under his share of the tarpaulin.

"Nothing much," replied Sam. "I was just thinking what a queer bunch women are."

"You can't blame me," said Ponto. "She used to be all right."

"I'm not blaming you, Ponto old boy. I'm not blaming anyone. No man is ever responsible for how a woman turns out. They're all the same; they start off okay but they change as sure as the weather does, only they're less predictable."

"What's that got to do with us sleeping out here on the ground?" demanded Ponto impatiently.

"Everything," said Sam. "You see, if we hadn't relied on a woman we'd have had a chance of working on something with more show of getting what we wanted. As soon as you gamble on a woman the odds are automatically against you. That's the way life is. It's always been like that, and always will be, I s'pose. The trouble is it's like looking into the sun; so obvious you can't see it."

"I don't get what you're driving at," said Ponto.

"Well look at it this way," said Sam. "Whenever a man runs into a bit of crook luck it's a quid to a broken bootlace that there's a woman behind it somewhere, because there's a woman behind everything. Otherwise there'd be nothing at all. We're stuck with them and the only thing a man can do about it is make allowances for them."

"Ar—they're not that bad," said Ponto sleepily. "You've just got a bee in your bonnet about 'em."

"Not that bad, eh?" said Sam. "Well what about that young tart over in Aussie? Good looking, plenty of cobbers, pots of dough; but that didn't stop her poisoning-off a boarding-house full of blokes, did it?"

"You can't judge them all by that one," said Ponto. "You're nuts! Women are okay."

"Yeah, they're all okay in their place all right," said Sam, "once it's dug for them."

"You're nuts," repeated Ponto. "Go to sleep."

Which Sam did, leaving Ponto to lie there staring for hours at the broken sky and wondering what he'd done to deserve such rotten treatment.

Sam and Ponto rose early that morning because railway workers do and they didn't particularly want to answer a lot of silly questions about their use of Government property. They breakfasted sleepily at a warm little shop near the station and then wandered around the streets waiting for the bus depot to open so they could enquire about buses and fares to wherever they decided to go.

Suddenly Ponto stopped and grabbed Sam's arm.

"Strike me pink!" he said, pointing through the thin crowd at a meandering figure that Sam had already noted as being distinctly unusual. "There's Toddy Dunn! Toddy! Toddy! Over here!"

Toddy

Toddy leaned absently on his favourite gate, watching the ragged tide of fern and scrub sneaking down the hillsides, through what was left of his disintegrating fences and into his paddocks. Rushes and weed were spreading across the rank, starved pasture from the swampy creek. The weedy in-bred survivors of his father's thousand Romneys stood scattered in little clusters, like headstones, along the rocky, scrubby face opposite.

Toddy Dunn, the farmer. Fifteen acres in grass, five acres in mud, sixty acres in scrub and not a standing chain of fence on the place. He'd swapped a cow for a heap of posts the year before. They lay in the grass by the boundary gate, which also lay in the grass.

Toddy Dunn. Somewhere between thirty and forty, with the kind of face you don't really notice till you've known him for a while, and odd wisps of hair sticking out under his found-on-the-road hat like frayed rope-ends. With clothes that would never fit him properly, no matter what size they were. Feet slopping around in gumboots two sizes too big for him because they only had tens left in the store when he bought them and the storekeeper always made him nervous. And the enormous oilskin coat he wore everywhere because it was better to be laughed at for wearing a big coat than for holes in your trousers.

Good old Toddy; never did anyone any harm in his life, nor any good. He'd do anything for you but you'd be a mug to let him. He'd be sure to make a mess of it or break something.

He glanced at the sad, sagging old woolshed that was once

the best in the whole district; and the great clump of wool-hung blackberry in the corner where the sheep-dip used to be, a grave for the cultivator—you could still see a shaft reaching up out of the tangled rigging of the vines, as though it were pointing at its murderer, or drowning. The mossy grey bones of the yards that Toddy and his brothers had split the rails for; and which stock agents had leaned upon, looking inscrutable, a long time ago.

A hell of a long time ago. Before the funerals and fern and borrowing off the bank and leaks and expenses and things breaking down and falling to bits all over the place. And messages left at the store by neighbours who could have come and told him, but didn't bother. And the Loan and Merc.

He trod a little drain in the mud to let the water out of one puddle into another and wondered where Bovo was, his brown dog Bovo, who thought Toddy was okay. Who listened to everything he said and didn't care that he hardly ever did any work. Not that Bovo was in a position to criticise, he was about as much use round the place as an extra blowfly. He was quite happy to follow Toddy around so long as he didn't go too fast or too far or ask him to work the cows or the sheep, or any of that kind of nonsense. And sometimes, like now, Bovo would get in under or behind something and hibernate for a day or two.

Toddy draped himself over the top rail of the gate, pulled the sleeves of his coat over his bony wrists in case anyone came, and worked out whether he should try calling the dog from where he was or go down to the gate and yell out there. It was too close to lunchtime to be worth going all the way down to the jetty, where he'd found Bovo last time, so he whistled a couple of times and went into the house to stoke up the fire. No wood.

He sneaked an armful of manuka from the clump near the house that he was saving for when he got too old to get his firewood from up the hill. He often did that these days. He built up a fire in the old stove that would have roasted the poker—lighting fires was one of the two things he could do efficiently—and had a feed of cold mutton sandwiches and tea without milk or sugar. By the time he'd read the "R.D.S." column in the *Weekly News* and rinsed out his mug it was nearly lunchtime. Half-past eleven, in fact.

About one o'clock he left the yard with a spade, a billy of assorted staples and a pair of fencing-pliers to fix a hole in the boundary fence he made for the neighbour's bull before the mortgage company took all his cows. Now the sheep were getting out. Not that Toddy minded them getting a feed wherever they could, but the neighbour didn't seem to be all that delighted about it. In fact Toddy had a pretty shrewd idea that some of his ewes were being fed to Willy Butcher's dogs.

Bovo came from one of his secret places and walked disinterestedly along in front so that Toddy had to slow down. But he would probably have slowed down anyway.

They crossed the creek on the log that had flooded down to replace the old swing-bridge two years before, and angled up the hill along sheep-trails through the manuka and rocks. Once or twice Bovo took the wrong track and then wouldn't admit it, working his way slowly back in a big semicircle to the track Toddy was on as though he'd meant to go that way all the time.

Toddy had a bit of trouble finding the right hole in the fence because a lot of manuka had grown up since he was there last. He started on a post-hole and found he'd dug it too far out from the fence, so he broke off some scrub and threaded it through the two wires that were left. There wasn't a post handy anyway. Then he sat on the tail of his coat and told Bovo a long story about nothing in particular that started somewhere in the middle and didn't have an ending.

He mentioned a big wife who went to bed in curling-pins and cream and bed-jackets and socks. And teeth in a mug and hot-water bottles. Smelling of Vicks VapoRub and flash soap. Who ate cake and nagged herself to death about Toddy not working very hard.

He mentioned his boy Joe, who only came home to wait till he could get another job, which he never seemed to look very hard for, or work very hard at when he got it.

He remembered the man from the Loan and Merc. who was coming next week to auction everything off because of mortgages and things. And he made a few plans for what he was going to do afterwards. Then unmade them. (Perhaps they'd ask him to stay on and manage the place.)

Then he thought up another couple of lines of a poem about Bovo he'd been working on; and Bovo thumped the ground a few times with his tail in approval.

After that things got a bit disjointed and an hour and a half before it was time to go home for afternoon tea he woke Bovo up and they wandered off down the hill, taking the spade for a walking-stick and leaving the tin of staples and the pliers for another time.

Because of it being a bit early Toddy decided to go and have a look at what the scrubcutter had done. The part of the gully that could be seen from the house had been cut roughly enough but the rest of it hadn't been touched. He'd been done! The man from the Loan and Merc. was going to worry himself sick over it. On the way back to the house Toddy decided that it mightn't be such a good idea to wait around for the Loan and Merc. man after all.

When he'd had a mug of cold tea and a little rest he went out and cut an extravagant pile of firewood from the best and closest manukas he could find. Enough to last four hours.

Then he went into the bedroom and wheeled out the old push-bike he'd perked off a neighbour who was leaving the district four years before. He leaned it against the sink ready for the morning and wiggled the wobble in the front wheel. It was a lady's bike so he kept his old Public Works shovel tied along the frame to make it look right. He used to wheel out bales of hay on it, which hadn't done the contraption much good, but it still worked.

With the fire bellowing up the chimney and yesterday's

stew heating on the cool end of the stove, there was just time for Toddy to go out and lean on the gate to watch the fern and the going-down sun.

The morning was fine and half gone when Toddy dragged on his gumboots at the door and went to cut down some mutton for Bovo, who wasn't up yet. Back at the house he left a note on the sink for the Loan and Merc. man about the scrubcutter and Bovo. Then he wheeled his bike out through the gently-steaming mud in the yard and down to the gate. Bovo didn't come to see him off, which made no difference to either of them. He mounted his bike and creaked and wobbled away down the clay road with sixteen quid in his oilskin pocket, no gear and no idea where he was heading.

Willy Butcher was working on his road fence but didn't even look up when Toddy rode past. Must have been feeling a bit guilty about Toddy's sheep—or wild about the holes in the boundary fence. When he came a bit further on to Willy's cottage by the roadside, Toddy stopped and let Willy's old cattle-dog go. Willy was always skiting how he just had to let the dog off the chain and it'd bring the cows in and hold them at the yard till he came to do the milking. Toddy buckled up the collar again to make it look as though it had been slipped and rode on down the road towards Jim Raggin's place.

Jim's was the last farm on the road they could bring cars and trucks to and he took messages for everyone further on—everyone, that is, except for Toddy. Raggin had known Toddy's father pretty well and didn't approve of the way Toddy had been handling the farm since the old man died. Furthermore, he was always pestering Toddy for a few miserable quid for a plough he'd borrowed and then lent to Willy Butcher, who'd broken it. And furthermore, old Raggin scared hell out of Toddy, so he rode past as fast as the bike would safely go and hoped he wouldn't be called out to.

The store was half a mile past Raggin's and the storekeeper

and Toddy had never been able to see eye to eye about money and things, so he didn't bother calling in.

The next farm was Cyril Bell's. Cyril used to be a cobber of Toddy's but old man Raggin had been getting at him lately and Toddy hadn't been able to borrow anything off Cyril for months. Cyril was splitting battens on a hill where he could see the road, otherwise the Taranaki gate between his heifers and his hay-paddock would probably have fallen down. He watched to see that Toddy went past his driveway before going on with his work.

That night Toddy slept in Len Roger's pumpshed, down at the bottom of the road where Stony Creek goes under the big bridge by the turnoff. He ate a couple of Len's turnips and washed them down with some of Len's cream from the stand by the gate.

When he pulled his bike out of the hedge next morning and went to lift it over a drain, the back wheel came off so he shoved everything back into the hedge and walked out on to the main road.

A few stray cars went past but none of them stopped to give him a lift because when he heard them coming he stopped and turned round to look and they couldn't tell which way he was going. And most of them thought he was a roadman, anyway. He somehow didn't like the idea of using his thumb. A bit of a shy bloke, Toddy.

So he just kept walking until a bloke in a truck who was going to Westport for a load of timber picked him up. This bloke wanted someone to talk to about what a hell of a time he was having with his brother-in-law, who was living with him and wouldn't get a job. He had some very definite and uncomfortable ideas about what ought to be done with people who were too lazy to get stuck into a decent day's work. He shouted Toddy a feed when they got to Westport because he was such a good listener and the bloke hadn't quite finished lamenting.

Toddy got in a few hours' sleep under a bridge on a river bank that night.

When the pubs opened he went into one of them and ordered a raspberry-and-lemonade on account of him not liking the look of Westport or the taste of beer, and the pub seemed the most likely place to pick up a ride down to the West Coast, where he'd heard nobody had to work very hard.

"Anyone going south?" he asked when there was a gap in all the conversations.

Everyone turned to look at him.

Of the eight people in the bar, four weren't going anywhere and the others all assured him that they were heading north. Even to Toddy it was obvious that at least two of them were lying. He had another drink and went across to the pub on the opposite corner.

"Sarsaparilla and lemonade," he said to the barman, for a change.

There weren't so many people in the bar but a couple of them looked like travellers.

"Anyone going north?" he asked loudly.

The chap nearest him turned quickly. "Yes," he said. "I can take you through to Murchison if you like."

Toddy looked around the bar with an uneasy look of a passenger who's not quite sure whether he's going to be seasick.

The chap moved along towards him. "We'll get away as soon as you're ready," he said. "I'll be glad of a bit of company on the trip, as a matter of fact. Makes the journey seem shorter somehow."

Toddy followed him out to a late-model car and got into the front seat beside him.

"You going right through to Murchison?" asked the man, starting up the car and letting in the clutch.

Toddy tried to think of somewhere along the road he could be going to, but couldn't.

"Yeah, right through."

"Good," said the man. And he began to talk, as though it

were true, of the high principles behind high-pressure advertising and salesmanship. He stopped when the car did, at Murchison.

That night Toddy slept in a tower of old tractor-tyres at a Ministry of Works dump. It was pretty cold, but not cold enough to prevent him from dozing off for almost an hour just before dawn.

Toddy In Trouble

A BIG TRUCK with a load of sheep rumbled and swayed along the country road, towing behind it a smouldering roll of grey dust that churned slowly in the still air and spread across the ferny roadside. The driver chopped her down a cog, drifted into a hollow and gunned her up the other side. Silence settled with the dust on the early-morning paddocks.

Toddy poked his head out of the dry culvert he'd spent the night in, cursed absently about missing a ride on the truck that had woken him up, and looked at the brightest part of the sky to see what kind of a day it was going to be.

Everything was country-grey and bleary. Weather that couldn't make up its mind. Everything windswept but not a breath of wind. Clouds, heavy and low as an early-morning eyelid, but no real signs of rain. A day that should have been cold but wasn't—it wasn't even warm instead. Not quite bleak; not quite anything. Just a dull, unfinished botchery of a day, left lying around to make things worse for him than they already were. The kind of day when truck-drivers are late and in a bad mood and won't even stop to give a bloke a lift. When the rasping of your boots on the dry gravel is like sandpaper and lemons for breakfast.

Couldn't rain even if it wanted to, he decided, trying not to notice a great blue bank of cloud that was happening in the sky to the west.

He climbed the overgrown bank on to the road. The only sign of the truck was a faint tail of dust dissolving on the horizon. He found a round stone and began kicking it along, wandering after it from one side of the road to the other.

No point in hurrying when you haven't got anywhere to go or anyone to run away from.

He thought of a little poem about atmospheres but only got as far as the third line because he couldn't think of a word that rhymed with circumstances and he didn't want to change the first line. It was such a good one.

Then it started raining the kind of rain you know is going to last all day. Big wet rain, bursting like applause on Toddy's oilskin, which was no better at keeping him dry than it was to look at. And he'd kicked a little split in the toe of one of his good gumboots.

For morning tea he had a lash at getting out to a cabbage-tree in a swamp because somebody had once told him the leaf-centres were good to eat. But all he got was his dry gumboot full of water. It was the wrong time of the year for cabbage-tree centres in any case.

For lunch he stood for a few minutes on a rise and watched the smoke breathing raggedly into the rainy wind from a farmhouse chimney. A comfortable-looking homestead, the kind of place where they have jars of pickles and plum jam, and hams hanging from hooks in pantry ceilings. He walked past the gate, deciding at the last minute not to go in and ask for something to eat.

The next place, he decided.

Half an hour's walking and four lines of a poem about old horses brought him to the next place. He switched off his mind and entered the gate into the driveway. It was further than he thought to the house with its tidy rows of standard roses and swept paths. He circled the place looking for a back door, and when he found it he changed his mind and went back to the front porch. His hand reached up and knocked on the door three timid times, as though he was afraid of breaking it. He noticed how dirty his hand was and put it away in his coat-pocket. Then he noticed the button of a door-bell and was just reaching out to push it when he heard footsteps coming. He just had time to get his hand out of sight again before the door was opened.

A woman, about thirty or so. Clean and ironed but smoking a cigarette like a man.

"What d'you want?" she asked in a voice like a nose-flute. Then she got a good look at him.

"Hell's bells," she whispered. Then, "You had an accident or something?"

There was a long pause while Toddy tried desperately to think of something to say, but he'd forgotten to turn his mind on again.

"Do you know a word that rhymes with mongrel?" he asked accidentally.

"Hell's bells!" repeated the woman loudly. She slammed the door and Toddy thought he heard her say, "He's nuts!" or something. He went back to the road and carried on walking. Not quite so hungry as he was before.

The rain stopped but obviously not for good. In fact it started again before all the water had leaked out of the boot with the hole in it.

On he went. Walking and hungry and wondering and hoping, and limping a little now because of a stone that wasn't worth taking his boot off for. He was too tired to think up a poem of his own so he just did a few alterations to one he learned at school.

Until he came to an old station homestead, spread-eagled in a drenched hollow by a muddy little creek, surrounded by puddles and rain and dog kennels and a long veranda. The woolshed, an implement shed and a pump shed stood like the three bears on a rise beyond. Everything painted the same colourless red. The name on the letter-box said Dan McDuff; and the voice that thundered at the barking dogs sounded like it. One of the dogs barked and seemed to laugh as Toddy walked up the drive.

"Well?" surprised a voice.

Toddy jumped. There was no one in sight.

"Well?" From behind a small, thick hedge emerged a small, thick man, as prickly as the privet. Dan McDuff without a doubt, a confirmed, convinced and convicted bachelor by the look of him.

Toddy was better with men than with women.

"Could you spare a drink a water," he said, asking for a feed.

"Well now," said the hedge-like farmer, "I could and I couldn't. Water's not cheap y'know. There's pipes and tanks and taps and hoses and pumps to be paid for, to say nothing of having too much of the stuff when you don't want it and too little when you do."

"Just a glass would be O.K.," said Toddy, asking for a drink of water.

"It'll have to be beer I'm afraid," said Dan McDuff. "I've been off water for years, ever since we had a smother up the back and the creek ran dry before it came down in a stinking flood. And you'll have to eat while you drink, because I'm hungry and I'm not going to eat alone. You're Toddy Dunn aren't you?"

Toddy almost jumped again.

"Your old man and I were in France together and were mates for years after. I can remember you as a kid. Come on up."

Dan McDuff fed him like a prodigal son and talked about Toddy's family as though they were his own. Then he slipped his mind back forty years while Toddy wasn't looking, and recalled Toddy's old man and himself as privates in lemon-squeezer hats, talking all the time about World War I as if the peace had only been signed the previous month. Toddy picked up some useful tips about walking duckboards, digging dugouts, avoiding shell-blasts and dodging snipers.

He could have stayed for a month but he realised that impossible questions demanding impossible answers would soon spoil everything. Over Dan's protests he headed off the next morning, saying he was on a walking holiday and would call back on his way home "in a couple of weeks".

Dan believed him and ordered another crate of beer on the strength of it.

As Toddy turned on to the main road he felt cheerier than he'd been for years. A poem about friendship jingled around in his mind all morning and he was so busy with it he forgot about cadging a ride.

He came to a little country store, where he bought biscuits and cheese and lemonade and a new pair of socks and found out that it was another eighteen miles to a place called Maruia, which he'd never heard of but apparently should have, so he didn't let on.

That night Toddy got into a paddock, chased a cow up off her warm patch and lay down to sleep curled up under his oilskin. Later he woke up freezing and chased another cow up. And so on, until a dog came to round them up in the morning. As he got through the fence on to the road Toddy thought he heard someone shouting at him, but he took no notice.

Toddy wasn't the type of bloke who paid over much attention to cleanliness. His beard was just getting long enough to be itchy. The rest of him was itchy for different reasons. But he fixed that. He stayed that night at the Hot Springs Hotel—in the hot springs. It was nice and warm and after he had sluiced his trousers and shirt and hung them up to dry he relaxed for the night in unaccustomed luxury. But towards morning he began to notice that something was wrong. He couldn't move. The long spell in the hot water had sapped his strength and he was as weak as a kitten.

It was his pants that had him worried most. They were hanging on a rock, just out of reach. He was going to need help again; and it was in the lap of the gods who was going to happen along first.

The old bloke who came pottering around just after daybreak looked as though he came from anywhere but the lap of the gods. Indeed, he was so scruffy-looking that Toddy had no hesitation in soliciting his assistance. He was the caretaker of the hotel grounds.

"Hey, mate," croaked Toddy in a voice he didn't recognise and that carried, at the maximum, fifteen feet.

The old bloke was about twenty yards away but he'd already seen Toddy's unhappy head sticking up out of his best little pool.

" 'Ere now. Wot's the caper, mate? Yer not supposed ter be in 'ere. A joker ought to top yer orf!"

"Could you pass me strides?" whispered Toddy.

"Git yer own blasted strides—and then git goin', before I gits the manager down 'ere!"

"I can't reach them."

The old bloke bent down and peered at Toddy.

"Y' crook?" he demanded.

Toddy nodded.

"Well y' better get outa there and give us a look at yer."

"I can't."

"Strike, mate," said the old bloke grabbing Toddy by the arm and heaving. "You blokes want to lay orf the meths. Y' could of drowned yerself. Yer better come down ter me 'ut. I got a drop of somethin' down there that'll put yer right in no time—'ere's yer breeks—'ell's teeth! Yer can't even stand on yer pins. You *are* in a bad way. 'Ere, let's give yer a hand. Easy now. You'll be right."

He helped Toddy down to his " 'ut" at the end of a row of cabins, sat him on the bed, jacked him up a meal of sorts, and poured him a dirty glass of home brew. "Guaranteed to sew yer up before yer kin git through the second bottle."

Toddy's ambitions lay elsewhere. He gradually subsided on the bed and the old chap did the decent thing and let him sleep his weariness off.

Some time during the afternoon Toddy woke up and looked around the hut. It was just a caretaker's hut, the same as any other caretaker's hut.

His oilskin was lying like a body across the foot of the bed. He put it on and went to the doorway. Somewhere a radio was playing but no one was in sight. He helped himself to a shave. His hands were so weak he could hardly hold the razor. As he was drinking his third jug of water from the tap by the door the old bloke arrived with two or three hundredweight of advice, which he summed up: "If yer can't take yer grog, lay orf it a bit. The beer won't do yer any 'arm but keep orf the top shelf and leave the plonk and the meths alone."

Toddy didn't mind being an alcoholic for the time being if it made the old bloke any happier. He grinned as roguishly as he could to match the old fellow's assumption, accepted his offer of a feed and a bed for the night, and began to feel that life had its compensations after all. The old bloke—"Call me 'Arold"—wasn't such bad company either and Toddy thought he could do worse than stay around for a day or two.

But in the morning, when 'Arold told him that the manager was due back from Christchurch, he realised that it would be a question of working or paying, and he decided to do neither. 'Arold saw him on his way with a packet of sandwiches and Toddy hit the road with as much regret as he'd felt in years.

The day was one of drifting, heavy showers. Then the rain stopped and a puddle of blue sky about the size of the Loan and Merc.'s house-paddock glowed clear as a young heading-dog's eye for a few minutes before the sun set. Just in time he found a perfect place to sleep. There was a new concrete water-trough standing on its side where it had been unloaded on to the bank beside the road.

He slept like a possum from a few minutes after he pulled the trough upside-down over himself until a few minutes before he discovered that he couldn't get out from underneath it next morning. It was too heavy for him.

He crouched there scratching bits of the Bovo poem on the inside of the trough with a stone until he heard voices and called out to a bunch of kids on their way to school, who only just heard him. They stood around for a while ignoring Toddy's suggestions that they help him lift one side of the trough so he could get out. They appeared to be much more interested in the argument about whose Dad they should go and get and who should get him. One of the younger boys was eventually bullied into it and off he went.

Dad was a long time coming and when he did he had a couple of other Dads with him

"Righto, you kids. Off you go now," he said in a sergeant-major voice. "This is no place for you!"

Then he banged on the trough with a stick or something. "Is anyone in there?"

"Yes, me," called back Toddy.

"What are you doing in there?"

"Trying to get out."

There was a muttered conference and suddenly the trough was heaved up and over, leaving Toddy blinking at the sudden light. The three men had sprung back as though they expected their mothers-in-law to pounce out at them.

Toddy got breakfast-on-the-porch off one of them and a ride on the back of a truck right over the Lewis Pass and down to Waikari with another, who didn't say what the trip was for or why Toddy couldn't ride in the front. The trip and nine lines of a poem about wind took nearly all day.

Two days later, in Christchurch, Toddy was wandering around with four quid in his pocket and the vague notion that he'd have to get a job soon or he'd be getting into difficulties, or something. He was heading for the West Coast when he started out from the Loan and Merc.'s farm and how he came to be in Christchurch was a bit confusing, but he supposed that Christchurch and he just happened to be in the same place, and left it at that. He wondered briefly how you went about getting jobs in cities and then decided to go to the pictures because he didn't want to think about it just yet.

Then, from somewhere behind or in front of him (or perhaps it was from across the road) came a staggering shout. . . .

T. Burke

The phone in the passage rang long-short-long. T. Burke took his feet out of the oven, stretched his legs twice each and put them back again.

West Coast Pub

THE LAST STRUGGLES of a water-logged sun had sunk into the gathering clouds, leaving the rain and wind to help themselves to the rest of the afternoon. Which they proceeded to do. Dank bush dripped and rattled all around and the road had become an endless succession of damp, blank corners. It was difficult to imagine that cars and trucks ever passed along it.

The smells and sounds of the city were a million miles away. Sam sloped along thinking about their last hangover, five lengths in front of Toddy, who was working almost silently on the third line of a poem about summertime. Ponto grumbled indignantly about "Whose bloody idea this was in the first place" half a furlong in the rear.

Sam suddenly stopped on a corner and waved to the others. They hurried along to see what it was and there in the middle of nothing much else was a solitary old pub that looked as though it had been put there by mistake.

"How's that for a beaut!" said Sam.

"Probably one of them there mirages," said Ponto ungraciously.

"You only get those in the desert," said Toddy.

"Do you reckon this is any bloody better than a bloody desert?" demanded Ponto.

"It is now," said Sam. "We might just hock a feed here, if we're lucky—or shall we carry on to the next place?"

"Ha, ha, ha!" said Ponto mirthlessly.

They went into a warm bar and stood with their backs to a small and smelly coal-fire. They were the only customers and the publican, without waiting to be invited, began pouring three beers.

"Nice day for it," said Sam pleasantly.

"Two bob," said the publican shortly, glaring across at the three men as though daring them to order anything other than what they were given.

Sam put a handful of change on the bar and Ponto grabbed the fullest glass, which was about two ounces short of full. The publican took half a crown, threw it savagely like a spear into the till behind him, and gave Sam threepence change out of his own money on the bar. Then he stood back with his massive arms folded, as though inviting a protest.

Ponto finished his first and put the empty glass back on the bar. The publican slopped half beer and half suds into the glass and took another two and six for his trouble. This time he didn't bother even pretending to give change.

"You two have got one to come," he said to Toddy and Sam. "If you can't handle an eight you want to drink five-ounce beers."

"We are," said Sam, but the publican's expression didn't change one way or the other.

"Any work going around here?" asked Ponto after a while.

"You might get old man Burke up the road here to give you a bit of post-splitting or something," grunted the publican. "He's always moaning about wanting work done."

"We'll give him a try in that case."

"Well don't bring any of his bloody cheques in here if you do," snarled the publican, rapping sharply on the bar with his beer-tap. Toddy slopped his beer and Ponto stepped a nervous pace or two backwards and glanced towards the door. Sam put his empty glass on the bar and said: "Well, we'll get on our way, shall we?"

But the publican had already seized a generous handful of the money and began to splash some beer into his glass. There was only two and tenpence left out of their last ten or twelve bob. Sam put the remaining coins in his pocket and said: "We'll make this the last one."

Ponto managed to time his drinking so they all emptied

their glasses together. They put them on the bar and turned to leave.

"Have one for the road," demanded the publican, starting to fill the glasses again.

The three men stopped and looked at each other. It was so quiet you could almost hear the beer going flat. The only time Sam had ever seen Ponto hesitate over the prospect of a glass of free beer.

"Well, thanks," said Sam leading the way back to the bar. "Good luck."

"That'll be two bob," announced the publican.

Sam put their last two bob on the bar and only just got his hand out of the way of the publican's descending paw in time.

"By the way," said Sam casually, "have you got a pen and paper I can borrow. My car has broken down back up the road and when these two chaps offered me a lift I forgot to get my brief-case out of it."

"Cost you sixpence," grunted the publican. "Not a charitable institution."

"Good," said Sam, putting the last sixpence on the bar.

The publican took the money and then rummaged under the bar, coming up with a ball-point pen and a rumpled old pad.

"Now," said Sam smoothing out the top sheet. "What is your full name please?"

"What, *my* name?" asked the publican, somewhat taken aback by this change in Sam's attitude.

"Yes, *your* name," said Sam impatiently.

"What do you want to know that for?"

"Come now, Mr Fry," said Sam, who had noted the name above the door as he came in, his invariable practice when sober. "You know who I am. Hasn't my department been in touch with you?"

"What department, Mr—er—?" The publican was apprehensive enough to resurrect a fragment of rusty courtesy. He carefully topped up all three glasses until they were so full even Ponto couldn't lift his without spilling a little beer.

"I'm a building inspector," explained Sam, as though he was talking to a backward child. "We're working in conjunction with the Hotel Licensing Commission. You know, of course, that we're closing down quite a few of the hotels on the Coast here."

"But they've already been here," said the publican. "They as much as said that my place would be left open."

"Unfortunately they've still to make their final decision," said Sam, making a careful note on the pad. "You must be one of the borderline cases because they've called for reports from us and the Department of Health. Now, what is your full name please?"

"Andrew Herbert Fry," said the publican meekly. "Look, I'm sorry if . . ."

"That's all right," said Sam, disinterestedly writing on the pad. "Now the full particulars of the hotel please—of course I'll want to check these things later but in the meantime I'll get as much information as I can from you for my report."

And Sam painstakingly filled four or five pages—while the publican filled their glasses—with information about the publican and his pub. Age, date and place of birth, where he came from, how long he'd been there, next-of-kin, wife, children, religion, political beliefs, education, previous occupations, donations to charities, medical history, debts, assets, monthly turnover, prices, overhead, renovations, mortgages, improvements, life insurance, depreciation, stock, profits, personal expenses, hobbies, weather, losses, pets, parking facilities, acreage, gardens, fences, orchards, fire insurance, wife's expenses, rats, mice, accommodation, lighting, toilets, heating, water, drainage, health measures, cutlery, employees, hours of business and "What's your criminal record?" concluded Sam.

"Nothin' much, nothin' much at all," squirmed the publican uneasily. By this time he was looking suitably subdued so Sam let it go at that and leafed thoughtfully through his notes.

"Your fire precautions are totally inadequate," quoted Sam from clause-something, section-something of the Fire Regulations Act, nineteen hundred and something. "We could close you down tomorrow. What measures do you intend taking?"

"I'll get on to it first thing in the morning," said the publican. "I'll order half a dozen of them fire-distinguisher things. I've been meaning to get on to it for a long time!" Sam gave him a disbelieving glance.

Another few agonising minutes of leafing through the notes and Sam closed the pad and handed the pen back to the publican. "That'll be all for the time being," he said. "You'll be hearing from us in due course. In the meantime I'd make several improvements to the place if I were you." He turned to Ponto and Toddy, who had been edging towards the door during the first half of Sam's interview and back towards the bar during the second half. "I think we'll get away," he said.

"Would you like to stay the night?" asked the publican.

"No thank you," said Sam curtly.

"Would you like another drink before you go?"

"No thank you," repeated Sam.

And the three travellers went out into drifting rain, leaving behind them the unhappiest publican on the West Coast.

"You just beat me to it," muttered Ponto dangerously, as soon as they were safely out of earshot of the pub. "I'd had just about enough of that thieving swine! You should have left him to me. I'd have dragged him over his bar and . . ." Ponto swung his right fist in a savage swipe at the air in front of him, went a little off balance, tripped on a stone and only just saved himself from falling flat on his face. "I'd have fixed him," he concluded a little lamely.

"He didn't seem to be very scared of you," observed Toddy. "It was Sam who had him worried."

"That's just because Sam got in first," said Ponto indignantly.

"Anyway, I didn't notice you sticking up for yourself!"

"Makes no difference," interrupted Sam. "There's only one way to deal with a bloke like that and that's to scare hell out of him. That's why I didn't want to stay there after we'd made our point. He'll be a worried boy for a few days now, wondering what's going to happen. He might think twice before he starts short-changing people from now on, too. These West Coast publicans are usually a pretty good team but there's a crookie in every bunch of blokes."

"Yeah," agreed Ponto. "But we fixed 'im!" And he was so excited about how "we fixed 'im" that he forgot to moan about having to keep up or where they were going to sleep that night.

"What was the name of that old bloke he told us wanted work done?" asked Toddy.

"Don't remember," said Ponto quickly.

"Bert, or something," said Sam. "We'll ask at the next place we come to. I think that's our best bet now. We'll have to give him a try—we're skinned!"

At this unsatisfactory turn the conversation had taken, Ponto began to fall behind the others and Sam continued talking to Toddy.

"Y'know," he said, "it's just a pity my old mate Harvey Wilson isn't with us. I remember once he and I set off with thirty bob in our kick and toured the whole country. We lived like lords for three months and hardly did a tap of work. Ah, those were the days." Sam shook his head fondly at the memory.

"Where did you get your money from?" asked Toddy, who didn't know he was about to be treated to one of Sam's yarns.

"Well I can't take any of the credit for that," replied Sam. "Y'see Harvey Wilson was a bit of a sharp businessman. Nothing crooked about him, mind you, but he could play more tricks with a torn quid than a monkey could with sixty feet of clothes-line.

"We were working on a Bailey bridge in the Waioeka Gorge

and one morning at smoko Harvey says to me: 'I think it's time we dragged our hook, Sam. It's about time a man had a little holiday. I can feel the itchy feet coming on.'

"'I'm a starter,' says I, 'but we'll have to pick up a bit of hay from somewhere. I've only got a quid left.'

"'And I've got ten bob,' says Harvey, 'but they owe us for two days' work. We'll be right.' Actually, we'd had a bit of a rough spin in a two-up game the night before and done our next week's wages in, but Harvey's memory was never the best about things like that.

"I'll say this for old Harvey, though, once he made up his mind about a thing he didn't waste any time. He got an urgent phone-call at lunchtime saying that his father was dying and he asked me to go with him for company to see the old boy for the last time. Real cut-up about it, he was. We drew our pay and spent the lot on a taxi into Rotorua. Spent a fortune on taxis in his time, old Harvey."

"What about his father?" asked Toddy.

"Oh that was just a phone-call about a load of shingle Harvey had accidentally sold for a bloke's driveway," said Sam. "Anyway, here we were in the Rotorua pub and Harvey says to me: 'Well Sam, here we go.'

"'We won't go far on the shingle money,' I tells him.

"'We'll go as far as we want to,' says Harvey. 'First we'll have a look at Auckland. I haven't been there for a year or two.'

"'How are we going to get there?' says I.

"'We might as well fly,' says Harvey. "And blow me down if we don't fly to Auckland that very afternoon. Harvey wrote out a chit for the airways people saying he was taking me up to Auckland to stand trial—I didn't know that till we got there. He didn't even tell them he was a detective, he just let them tell each other and we were quids in. Though I got a few funny looks out of them."

"You'd have gone for a skate if they'd caught you out," said Toddy.

"You wouldn't get away with it today," agreed Sam, "but

things were a lot slacker in those days. Anyhow, the first thing we did when we got to Auckland was look up a politician Harvey had heard about, in the phone-book. We went out there in a taxi and Harvey tells the lady he's a house re-blocking expert and does she know her house is sinking badly in one corner? He said he just happened to notice it as he was passing by and thought he'd drop in to let them know.

"Well, we got the job. Seventy-five quid to re-block the whole corner of this flash house. We moved in the next day with a hired truck full of hired gear and sat under there hammering and banging and scraping and generally filling in time between cups of tea and scones to make it sound right. Harvey trimmed the sides off some of the wooden piles to make them look like new ones. Then we splashed tar over everything to keep out the termites, and anybody who got the idea of having a close look at the job. We threw a few shovelfuls of dirt and chips on their flash lawn for effect and collected our dough. Took us two and a half days altogether —we had to get out before Friday, when the M.P. got home from Wellington.

"We cut the seventy-five quid out in great style and then Harvey takes us for another taxi ride. This time it was trees. He bowls up to a big old house and tells two old ladies he's a tree-felling expert and the big tree in their yard—it was a forty-foot pohutukawa—was rotting the guttering, causing dry-rot and damp-rot in the wall of the house, breeding mosquitoes, and goodness knows what. By the time he'd finished he had them convinced that if something wasn't done straight away they'd be paying out hundreds of quid for everything from new window-frames to hospital expenses. We got the job allright. Forty quid.

"Next day we hired a ladder and another truck and backed it through the hedge on to the lawn, and such shouting of directions, chopping of branches, placing of ropes and making of messes you never did see. Old Harvey could make posting a letter look like launching a rocket, once he got cracking. That job took us three and a half hours, not counting cups of tea. Then we shifted camp down to Napier, where Harvey hadn't been for a couple of years.

"In Napier," continued Sam, "Harvey paid ten quid for a condemned scow that had to be towed out to sea and sunk after it had been stripped. The cost of having it towed away and sunk had been estimated at twelve hundred quid so nobody had been game to touch it, but that didn't worry Harvey. We sold the fittings, as is—where is, for two-fifty quid and then Harvey donated the hulk to the Navy for a target. He got a personal letter from one of the nobs in the Navy, thanking him for his donation and commending his interest in the defence of our country.

"In Wellington we bought advertising space on the side of a new building and sold the lease to a big firm for seventy-five quid profit. That took us an hour and a half.

"In Christchurch we bought an option on some tramlines they wanted shifted for twenty quid, and Harvey sold the contract to a scrap-metal firm for a hundred quid.

"In Dunedin we bought up a big pile of broken telegraph poles for fifteen quid. They were supposed to be shifted but we cut them up into strainers and blocks and stays and sold them back to the Post and Telegraph Department for three quid each. We cleaned up a packet on that one, I can tell you.

"Strike, Toddy, I could go on for hours about old Harvey. He wasn't a crook or anything; too honest for that. But when it came to digging up a fast quid he couldn't be beat!"

Toddy had no doubt that Sam could have gone on about old Harvey for hours, and he might have done, had they not at that moment rounded a corner and seen what might have optimistically been called a farm, splattered raggedly amongst the swamp and bush on the Southern Alps side of the road.

On Contract

THE NAME, which looked as though it had been written with a yard-broom dipped in number-plate yellow paint in front of a tea-chest on the bank, was almost unmistakably T. Burke.

"This looks like the place," said Sam. And they stood for a few moments in the gateway, looking across low hills to where the Southern Alps, covered with cloud and snow, stuck up out of an irregular band of bush only a mile or two away. T. Burke's unfenced driveway twisted itself through the stumps and logs of an unfenced paddock to an unpainted house behind an untrimmed hedge on a rise two hundred yards back from the road. Toddy felt at home almost at once.

They climbed the broken steps on to a back porch littered with gear and Toddy was delighted to see an oilskin almost exactly the same as his own, only older, hanging there. This was his line of country. He stepped forward and knocked loudly on the door. Then he stepped back and got behind Sam as flooring creaked inside the house.

A little chap as unkempt as his farm opened the door and dragged it noisily through the groove the bottom corner had worn in the floor. An active-looking bloke, wearing a holey jersey and a baggy pair of long red underpants. His face was so wrinkled that he looked like a weather-beaten bloodhound. He stood there squinting at his three visitors, arms hanging at his sides, the fingers slightly bent as though round an invisible axe-handle. An authentic, rugged, backblocks New Zealander. Ponto didn't like the look of him at all.

"You Mr Burke?" asked Sam.

"Yeah, that's me," said the little bloke, in the hardest-working voice Ponto had ever heard. "What kin I do for yer?" He grinned to show four teeth the colour of well-smoked ham and spat expertly through a small gap between Ponto and the corner of the porch. Ponto stepped back on to a loose step and clutched wildly at the doorway to save himself from falling.

"How about these posts of yours?" asked Sam.

"They're okay."

"Well, do you want anybody to split them?"

"No, not yet. You want to have a go at it?"

"Yeah, we'll look the job over."

T. Burke ran a hand like a crayfish claw through his going-grey hair and said: "I suppose you'll want to have a look at the timber. Hang on till I get me boots on." He pulled his socks further on to his feet and shoved them into a pair of mud-caked boots on the porch. Then he led the way out through a little side-gate in the hedge.

"Hey, what about your strides?" said Ponto.

"What about 'em?"

"Aren't you going to put any on?"

"Nar, not worth it. They're torn anyway and we've only got to walk as far as the tractor."

So in his long, baggy underpants T. Burke led them through the mud to a rusty, corrugated-iron shed, in which was parked a small crawler tractor with a sledge hooked on to the tow-bar.

"How are you going to back her out with the sledge on?" asked Toddy as they approached the shed.

"Worked that one out years ago," chuckled T. Burke, looking around at the three men as though he had invented sledge and tractor. "Knocked the other end out of the shed."

And he had—with the tractor, by the look of it.

Ponto, Toddy and Sam stood looking around while T. Burke pottered back and forth between the crank-handle and the carburettor until the tractor started.

"Hop on!" he shouted, climbing unhurriedly into his seat at the controls.

They crowded awkwardly on to the sledge, were jerked

out through the jagged hole in the end of the shed and dragged off down a muddy track through T. Burke's stump-studded paddocks—or paddock, the only sign of a continuous fence being along the road.

A few straggly groups of bedraggled sheep picked around among rotting logs, stumps and fern. Sam noticed a resemblance between the sheep and T. Burke himself. The same damp-raggedness.

They came to a gate in a cutting, which Toddy opened and then closed behind them. There was no fence either side of the gate, just the gate itself stuck in the middle of the track.

"Going to fence all this one day," explained T. Burke as Toddy climbed back on to the sledge. "Put in the gate last year."

They carried on along the track, which took them round the side of a hill above a long swamp. The tractor stopped suddenly and they nearly fell over the front of the sledge.

"This'd be as good a place as any to make a start," said T. Burke, shutting off the motor and looking round at them.

"Where's the bush?" asked Sam.

"No bush. Just these logs lyin' around here. Some pretty good timber in amongst it too, if you ask me."

"Where?"

"Well I found a nice lump of white pine in the fern down the side here when I went to get a sheep that was hooked up a couple of months back. There's probably more of it lyin' around. You never know what you might come across once you start pokin' about."

"But white pine's no good for posts, is it?" said Toddy.

"Isn't it?"

"No," put in Sam. "It rots as quick as you put it in the ground."

"Is that a fact now? What's it like for battens?"

"It's okay for battens."

"That's all right then. You can knock it up into battens. No sense in wasting the stuff."

Toddy, Ponto and Sam stood on the little sledge looking around. T. Burke sat leaning on the steering-clutches of his tractor and a sheep bleated on the opposite hillside.

"Shall we go down and have a look at it now, or leave it till tomorrow?" said T. Burke, glancing at the overcast sky. "I think we're in for a bit of dirty weather if you ask me."

"I think we'd better leave it till tomorrow," said Ponto quickly. "We haven't got our working-gear on."

"Okay," said T. Burke. "We'll have to go along here for a fair way to turn round. I'll give the tractor a crank."

"I'll wind her for you," said Toddy, taking the crank-handle T. Burke was pointing at him. He had to walk through the mud on his heels so the water wouldn't leak in the holes in the toes of his gumboots.

They carried on along the track for another half-mile before T. Burke found a place to turn his tractor. The country was the same everywhere they looked, rolling hills of burnt-over bush with fern and blackberry and swamp in all directions. Here and there were black stains, like old bomb-blasts in the bush, where T. Burke had tried unsuccessfully to burn off the scrub.

Back at the house T. Burke climbed off the tractor and said: "Just about earned ourselves a cup of tea. I hope the fire hasn't gone out."

He led them into the kitchen.

"Don't take any notice of the place. It's a bit rough. Mum's been away for a while."

The kitchen smelled strongly of methylated spirits, rank butter and wood smoke. Two mantle-lamps swung from hooks in the ceiling, across which were several big stains where the roof had been leaking. Against one wall was a set of floor to ceiling shelves, held in place by a piece of fencing-wire stapled to the wall on either side. There was hardly space for another pile of magazines or box of nuts and bolts on the shelves, and all the food that wasn't littering the big table under the window by the back door, seemed to be piled around a big old clock on the mantelpiece above the wood-stove. One end of the mantelpiece was reserved for tins of kerosene and bottles of meths for the lamps, while the other held a shoe-box overflowing with bills and receipts, odd bits of paper and a handful of loose .303 and shotgun cartridges. The weapons themselves leant in the corner behind the door.

T. Burke got a couple of pieces of totara out of the box by the stove and began to split them on the hearth with a five-pound axe. The piece of wood along the front of the hearth was chopped nearly through.

"Sit down," said T. Burke. "I'll just get the fire stoked up. You can't beat a cup of tea when you come in from working."

They found chairs round the room and sat looking at each other in silence.

Toddy noticed a mouldy old coat lying on a heap of newspapers in a corner. It stood up, stretched itself, waved its tail and lay down again. It was a mouldy old dog. Too tired even to bark at strangers.

"How long has your wife been away?" Sam asked, to make conversation.

"She went to spend the week-end with her sister in Invercargill and hasn't come back yet—must be enjoying herself. She's been there close on eleven years now."

He lit the fire he'd set in the stove and a cloud of smoke billowed out around him until he could hardly be seen.

"She smokes a bit when the wind's from the north," he explained philosophically, scraping kettles and pots around on the stove. "She'll settle down after a while. I suppose you chaps must be hungry. I'll heat up this stew."

The smoke slowly filled the room.

"Are you sure your chimney's not blocked?" coughed Ponto.

"Don't think so. She caught fire and burned herself clear about a year back. Shouldn't be choked up again yet."

They had a brew of strong tea and a plate of mutton stew each, with slices of bread and butter. Then T. Burke filled and lit the lamps while Sam stacked the dishes in the sink, poured boiling water from the kettle over them and left them to steam dry on the bench. T. Burke was evidently no hand at the dish-washing game but he showed Ponto and Toddy a bedroom—"This do you fellers?"—that was fitted out with camp-stretchers for use as shearers' quarters. There was a bathroom at the end of the passage near the kitchen but you couldn't get the door open properly.

They sat in the smoky kitchen. T. Burke began puffing on a putrid old pipe. The phone in the passage rang two shorts and a long, but T. Burke didn't take any notice of it, so it can't have been his ring.

"Got a good price for the wool last year," he explained, "so I thought I'd get a bit of fencing done. Once I get the place cut up into paddocks I can winter more stock."

"How many acres have you got?" asked Sam.

"Two thousand—but only about half of it's any good. The rest needs draining and clearing."

"What are you paying for the post-splitting?"

T. Burke thought laboriously for a while and then said, "I'll give you a tenner a hundred and your keep. How's that? I'll supply the gear."

They all agreed on the price and Ponto started skiting how he used to split a hundred posts a day on his own. Sam, who Ponto thought had never swung an axe in his life, said nothing and Toddy leafed through a copy of Henry Lawson's collected works he'd found on the mantelpiece. When the big clock gonged out eight o'clock T. Burke put his old dog outside and reached up to unhook one of the lamps.

"Think I'll turn in," he said. "You blokes can sit up if you feel like it. Do you know how to turn the lamp off?"

"Yes thanks," said Toddy, "I'll fix it. What time are we getting up in the morning?"

"There's no need to be too early. I'll give you a call when I've got the fire going."

"Okay. Good night."

"See you in the morning."

"G'night."

He took his lamp and creaked off up the passage to his bedroom. After a few moments of silence Sam said: "Well, what do you think of it?"

"Looks pretty good to me," said Toddy. "How about you, Ponto?"

"Well I don't know," replied Ponto slowly, looking at nothing on the table in front of him.

"What do you think of the timber?" asked Toddy.

"We haven't seen it yet. But it'll be a bit hard to get at."

"Yeah. We mightn't be able to make it pay," said Ponto hopefully.

"We'll have to knock out a couple of hundred posts to get some money," said Toddy.

"You're right there," agreed Sam. "What say we talk it over again in about a week's time?"

"Good idea. We'll just play along in the meantime."

No one had anything to add to the conversation so they took the lamp into their bedroom and sorted out their stretchers. There were pillows and blankets stacked in the corner and they were able to make up quite comfortable, musty beds for themselves. Toddy took off his oilskin and spread it over his bed, said good night to the others and turned off the lamp. He lay in the darkness wishing he'd had T. Burke for a neighbour and listening to the house creaking and settling down for the night. He went to sleep to the sound of rain hissing on the iron roof; and awoke an hour later to the sound of it splattering on to his oilskin. He got up and shifted his camp-stretcher. The clock in the kitchen struck twelve as he settled back to sleep again.

They were all awake when T. Burke travelled the creaking passage an hour after daylight and chopped his kindling on the hearth. The rain had stopped but water still chuckled in the guttering and splashed into a full drum under the spouting outside. A pool of water on the floor where Toddy's bed had been, drained out under the door into the passage.

"Been raining," observed Sam, yawning.

"Yes," said Ponto quickly. "It might be too wet to work today."

Toddy got up, put on his oilskin and his gumboots and went out into the kitchen.

"In for a dirty day," said T. Burke from behind a cloud of smoke at the stove.

"Looks like it," said Toddy.

"Coming from a bad quarter. We'll probably get a few days of it now."

Sam went out and stood on the porch. The sky was the black-grey colour of T. Burke's hair and just as untidy-looking. Four soggy sheepskins had blown off the clothes-line so he let down the prop and hung them up again. Then he got an armful of firewood from a lean-to on the wash-house and took it into the kitchen.

"Thanks," said T. Burke. "What's it look like outside?"

"Not the best. I don't think we'll get much done today."

Toddy came into the kitchen and Ponto started heaving on the bathroom door, which shook the whole house.

"How did you sleep?" asked T. Burke.

"Like a log," answered Toddy. "What's the weather going to do?"

T. Burke crossed to the window and said, "You see that hill out there?"

"Yeah," said Toddy, peering at the mist-covered outline of a low hill T. Burke was pointing at.

"When you can see that hill it's going to rain. And when you can't see it, it's raining."

Toddy was still trying to work that one out when T. Burke slid a mug of hot tea across the table to him. Ponto came in looking no cleaner and inspected the rim of his mug before drinking from it.

"I was thinking," said T. Burke. "I've got quite a few odd bits of this and that I need a hand with round the place. I'll pay you seven bob an hour to dig a few chains of drain and tack one or two boards on the sheep-yards and things like that. It'd do to fill in time in showery weather when it's not worth going out to the posts."

"Suits me," said Sam, glancing at Ponto and Toddy, who nodded their agreement. "You can show us what you want done after breakfast."

"Where's the old dog?" asked Toddy, looking around the kitchen.

"Oh he'll be out in the tractor-shed," explained T. Burke. "He stinks a bit too much when he gets wet so he has to stay outside when it rains."

While they were piling the dishes in the sink it began to rain steadily so they all relaxed. Ponto tried not to look pleased, and failed completely.

"She's set in for the day all right," announced T. Burke. "We might as well make ourselves comfortable."

He pulled his chair up to the stove, put his feet in the oven and settled himself comfortably behind an old copy of the *Journal of Agriculture*.

Sam went out and split a few blocks of wood while Ponto did the dishes. Toddy followed T. Burke's example and dozed off in a chair. The phone in the passage rang three longs.

Sam cooked up some mutton chops he found in the safe for lunch. They had to wake T. Burke up to eat. It was still raining.

After Toddy had stacked the dishes on the bench to dry, T. Burke stood up and said: "Think I'll do a bit of washing."

He peeled off his long underpants, rinsed them through in the sink, wrung them out and put them back on again. Then he sat in his chair by the fire to dry them.

Ponto was horrified. He kept looking back and forth between the sink and T. Burke's steaming figure in front of the stove.

They read old newspapers and magazines all afternoon and T. Burke went to bed at his usual eight o'clock. As soon as he'd gone Ponto burst into song.

"Did you see that!" he cried. "The dirty old coot. Washing his bloody underpants in our sink!"

"His sink," corrected Toddy.

"We've got to eat out of it," said Ponto.

"Do we really?" laughed Sam.

"It's no bloody laughing matter," said Ponto. "The dirty old coot. He's just a dirty old coot," he repeated.

"Dirty," said Sam, "he's not dirty. He's just a bit rough, that's all. If you want to see a real dirty bloke I can put you on to any amount of them. Blokes that'd make Burke look like stainless steel.

"There's old Hubcap Harry, the roadman from Taranaki, for example. Picks up anything he finds run-over on the road, from hedgehogs to hawks, and cooks them up on the side of the road in hubcaps he snicks off people's cars with his shovel, while he's giving them directions. I've seen dogs turn up their noses at better tucker than some of the stuff Harry used to eat at times.

"He lost one of his gumboots once, but he got his money's worth out of the one he had left. He took it to work full of cold tea every day for months till it sprang a leak on him. Then he used to carry his lunch in it. Reckoned it saved paper. The last time I saw old Harry he was using the top of that gumboot for a hat and the toe part to keep his tobacco in.

"Then there was another old bloke. Super-bag Simpson, they called him. Nobody could remember his real name, he'd been called Super-bag for so long. Used to wear nothing but pants, boots and a super-bag with neck and armholes cut in it, summer or winter, rain, hail, or shine. He lived in a little hut out the back of a sheep-station I was on up the North Island and he was never known to have a wash in his life. Reckoned he belonged to some secret religion you had to be born into and the members weren't allowed to wash, ever. But no one ever saw old Super-bag go to church or do any praying.

"In the finish they couldn't get anyone to take gear or

tucker up to Super-bag's hut because of the smell. Everything had to be left in a big box on the side of the track and Super-bag would pick it up later. They reckon you could smell his hut from the homestead on a clear night. He fair stank, did old Super-bag. They were worried about what was going to happen when he died, there was no one game enough to go up and bring him out. In the end the station shepherds all cleared out and got other jobs, so they wouldn't have to face Super-bag, alive *or* dead. There was a real dirty bloke for you.

"And then there was Ergot Ernie, an old World War One bloke who used to make the odd quid picking grass-seed. Taught me the game when I was just a young feller, but I had to turn it in after a few weeks. One day I came across old Ernie scoffing a half-cooked magpie he'd shot. Reckoned he'd run out of grub and offered me a leg, but that wasn't a good enough excuse for me. Put me off my tucker for days.

"They had to lock Ernie up a few years later. Somebody found him living in a cave on the coast—living on seagulls, mussels and pauas, raw ones. Great feast he was having himself. They reckon his brains had slipped out of gear, poor coot.

"There's plenty of those blokes around but it makes me sad talking about the poor sods. It's not their fault really. They just get that way with age and habit, I s'pose. But there's no need to worry about Burky. There's nothing wrong with him."

"I still reckon it's a dirty trick," said Ponto.

"Ar, forget it," said Toddy. "It's not worth worrying about."

"Let's hit the sack," said Sam, "so we'll be nice and fresh for a good day's work tomorrow."

But as Toddy led them up the passage with the lamp, Ponto was heard to mutter: "Work! Work for that dirty old coot!"

An Inside Job

IT WAS STILL RAINING next morning when T. Burke got up and creaked his coughing way along the passage to the kitchen. Then there was a long, smashing crash that sat Toddy, Ponto and Sam upright in their beds.

"Where are y'?" yelled T. Burke.

They ran up the passage and crowded into the kitchen doorway behind T. Burke. The clock and all the things that had surrounded it on the mantelpiece lay in a scattered heap on the floor. The prop from the clothes-line was hanging by one end from a piece of string tied to a nail behind the passage door.

"Who done that?" demanded T. Burke.

"Done what?" asked Ponto.

"Someone put the end of that pole to the door here and left the other end resting on the end of the mantelpiece. When I opened the door it slid along the wall at the back of the mantelpiece and shoved everything off. Now who done it?"

"Would it be one of the neighbours?" suggested Sam.

"What the hell would me neighbours want to do that for?" T. Burke turned accusingly on Ponto. "You've busted me mother's clock!" he said.

"Here, cut that out," cried Ponto indignantly. "I never done it."

"Then who did? Where's Toddy?"

Toddy came back along the passage putting on his oilskin. "Don't look at me," he said. "I wouldn't do anything like that."

"Then it must have been you," said T. Burke, turning on Sam.

"It wasn't me, Burky. Are you sure somebody round here hasn't got it in for you?"

"No, they haven't. Nothing like this ever happened before. It must have been one of you blokes."

"You're way off the beam," said Sam. "We wouldn't do a thing like that. No sense in it."

"I suppose you jokers think I made this mess myself!" said T. Burke. He turned to Toddy.

"It wasn't you who done this?"

"No it wasn't. I already told you that."

"And it wasn't you?" said T. Burke to Ponto.

"That's right, it bloody wasn't," said Ponto defiantly.

"And it wasn't you either, I don't suppose?" he asked Sam.

"For the third time, no," said Sam.

"Then you didn't all have a hand in it?"

"Nope."

"No."

"No."

"Well it must have been somebody," said T. Burke grimly, "and if I ever find out who it was they're going to be sorry for it."

He knelt by the scattered pile of things around the smashed clock and began sorting the broken from the unbroken.

Sam picked up the end of the clothes-prop from the floor and placed it on the mantelpiece to try it out. The others watched as he opened and shut the door several times. The pole slid neatly back and forth along the mantelpiece.

"Whoever worked that one out had his head screwed on," he said quietly.

"He'll have his head screwed off, if I get my hands on him," muttered T. Burke.

Toddy lit the fire and they drank tea and ate toast in a strained silence. Outside the wind threw armfuls of rain against the house and roared in the chimney. The phone in the passage rang short-short-long.

After breakfast Sam heated water in pots on the stove to

have a bath and T. Burke concentrated on tying up holes in his socks and trousers with string.

Toddy and Ponto swapped magazines back and forth across the table. Nobody spoke much all morning.

In the afternoon the rain stopped for an hour and they went outside to have a look at what needed doing to T. Burke's sheep-yards. Sheets of water lay in the hollows, and creeks and drains ran bankful and muddy. The old sheep-dog shook himself in the barn doorway and blackbirds chickered frantically in the hedges.

The woolshed had been out of use for some years for lack of attention and repair and T. Burke got his twelve-hundred-odd sheep shorn in a neighbour's woolshed each year. But he used his yards occasionally, or the four pens of them that would still hold sheep.

They discussed dismantling one half of the yards for timber to fix the other half with until it began to rain again and they went inside.

The atmosphere was still a bit ragged and it was with a very brief grunt and a useless glance at the broken clock on the mantelpiece that T. Burke took his lamp and bade them good night, shortly after tea.

After he'd gone there was a short silence into which Sam said: "She's a grim business."

"Grim all right," agreed Ponto. "Fancy the old sod blaming us. After washing his underpants in the sink, too."

"There wouldn't be anyone else hanging around here, would there?" Toddy asked Sam.

"I don't think so. What beats me is that whoever it was must have been sneaking around in the house and that's not easy to do without making a racket, the way the floor and doors are. They'd have to go outside for the clothes-prop, for one thing, and the back door makes enough noise to wake the dead."

"It's got me beat," said Ponto helpfully.

"What about the windows—or the front door?" asked Toddy.

"He's got the front door nailed up and there isn't a window in the place that wouldn't fall out if you touched it," said Sam. "I had a good look round today while Burky was outside cutting wood. There's only one way in and out of here and that's by the back door."

"Doesn't look like there's anything we can do about it then," said Ponto.

"We can keep our eyes and ears open," said Sam. "And above all, keep on the right side of old Burky. If he blows his top and shows us the gate we've had it. Apparently jobs are as scarce as fences round here and we're stuck with this one till we make enough money to move on."

"Well, I'm going to bed," said Ponto. "If I hear anyone roaming around in the night I'll be on to them like a ton of bricks."

"Think I'll come too," said Sam.

Toddy grabbed the lamp and led the way up the passage.

Then he lay awake in the dark for a long time, thinking around a poem about shearing. The old house creaked and rumbled but it was only the wind, and T. Burke snoring raucously in another room. The rain blew away on the last of the wind and left a clear sky for the morning.

T. Burke stalked warily along the passage and opened the door into the kitchen very slowly. Nothing happened, so he entered the room and began to split the kindling. Toddy and Sam got up to help and to talk about the weather. Ponto came into the kitchen shortly after the tea was poured and tried not to take any notice of all the talk about work that was going on.

They decided to tackle the sheep-yard job and clean it up in one day. Breakfast was bolted standing and the dishes left unwashed on the bench.

T. Burke passed a saw, two hammers, a box of nails and

staples, and a coil of number eight fencing-wire out of the woolshed.

Once the gear and the men were assembled at the job there was a unanimous slackening of the pace.

"We'll have to work this out," said T. Burke vaguely.

And they talked for an hour about how they were going to dismantle the old yards. Then T. Burke went back to the house to put the kettle on while Sam knocked four rails off the posts and Ponto carried them the thirty feet to where they were going to be used again, and sat down. Toddy rubbed his way gently with T. Burke's handsaw through a nail and a piece of wood that didn't need cutting. T. Burke's old dog wandered aimlessly around getting in the way.

After smoko, which took three-quarters of an hour, they went back to the job and knocked eight more rails off the old pens and stacked them by the ones that were to be fixed. By that time T. Burke had lunch ready. During what was left of the afternoon T. Burke had to go all the way down to the gate on his tractor to get a load of stuff. He took Toddy to help him load it on to the sledge, leaving Ponto and Sam to carry on with the work.

The "stuff" he had to pick up was three loaves of bread, a newspaper and a final notice to clear the ragwort off his road paddock. On the way back he had to stop and do something mysterious to the tractor and it was time to start putting dinner on by the time he and Toddy got back to the house.

Sam and Ponto had dismantled two more panels of the yards, taken a gate off its hinges, and put all the tools away in the shed by the time T. Burke called out for them to knock off.

After tea they sat round in the kitchen saying how these things took time, Rome wasn't built in a day and it was better to take your time and do a job properly than to rush in and make a botch of it.

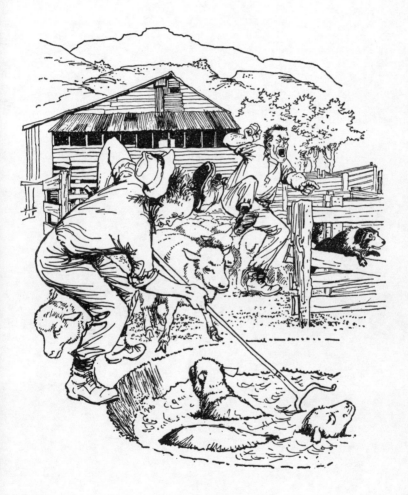

Crook Boots

THE NEXT MORNING it looked as though it might rain again later, so T. Burke suggested that they open up the drain behind the tractor-shed to let the water away from the sea of mud the tractor had churned up.

They gathered, an hour after breakfast, at the place where the drain had once been, with two spades, a shovel and a long piece of wire, which T. Burke said might come in handy.

T. Burke said they should start the drain from the top. Sam said it should be started at the bottom. Toddy said it didn't make any difference and Ponto said they should leave it till tomorrow. Then T. Burke went off to get a ball of string to peg out where the drain was to be dug and didn't come back until it was time to put the kettle on for smoko.

By lunchtime Sam had dug about six feet of the drain, which filled with water, so they decided to abandon the job until the place dried out a bit.

After lunch T. Burke climbed dangerously up the cluttered shelves and found a pack of cards. They played poker for staples all afternoon because it looked as if it was going to start raining any minute. By teatime it still hadn't rained.

"I'll have to ring up for some stores," said T. Burke. "They drop the order at the gate on Thursdays."

"What are we going to do tomorrow?" asked Sam. "If it's fine," he added.

"We'll have to kill a hogget for meat before we do anything else," said T. Burke. "That was the last of the mutton we had for tea."

It rained spasmodically through the night but by morning

there was hardly a thunder-cloud in the sky. After breakfast T. Burke took Ponto and his old dog and went off to bring a sheep into the yards from among the stumps and fern beyond the old woolshed. They stalked up on a bunch of half a dozen sheep in a hollow and saw that there were two hoggets and four ewes.

"One of those hoggets'll do us," whispered T. Burke. "We'll yard the whole bunch and pick out the fattest."

He put his old dog out round the sheep and the three of them managed to get the little mob headed for the yards. Toddy and Sam were waiting to help guide them into T. Burke's one good pen, but Toddy was standing too close to the gate. The sheep broke off across the paddock and the old dog couldn't catch up to them. So they went inside for morning tea to let the sheep settle down for a while.

It was nearly mid-day by the time they'd got a bunch of sheep yarded up. Then they found that what T. Burke thought were wether hoggets were in-lamb ewes.

"What's the difference?" asked Ponto.

"Nothing really," replied T. Burke. "One of these'll do us."

After lunch T. Burke got out the bread-knife and they went back to the yards to slaughter one of the ewes. Sam killed it, they all helped to hang it up on a gambrel in the woolshed doorway, and Toddy and T. Burke took it in turns to hack the skin off and dress the carcass. Ponto dug a far-too-small hole for the guts. By the time they'd finished T. Burke said it was too late to go down to the gate for their stores so they got the tools out, knocked four more rails off the old pen, put the tools away and went inside to put on a mutton stew for dinner. The old ewe turned out to be as tough to eat as she was to catch.

Toddy woke up first in the morning and listened for rain and T. Burke going up the passage. There was no rain but T. Burke went past at his usual time and rattled the handle of the kitchen door.

Then he gave a shout, which was cut off by a rending crash

that shook every timber and sheet of iron in the whole house. Toddy, Ponto and Sam leapt out of bed and ran to see what had happened.

The whole set of shelves, on which almost everything in the kitchen had been stacked, hung or leaned on, had crashed to the floor. Broken plates, cups, jars, books, boxes of bolts and nails, tins of food, and pots lay scattered everywhere. T. Burke was picking himself up out of a corner. He stood silently looking at the wreckage for a few moments.

"The shelf's fallen down," he said.

"Are you hurt?" asked Sam.

"No, the shelf hit the door just as I was going through it and knocked me out of the way."

"This has been rigged up," announced Ponto. "Look here."

A length of string was tied from the door handle on to the shelves. The piece of fencing-wire which had held them up hung from one of its staples. The other end had been undone.

"Someone," said Ponto, "has taken the wire off this end of the shelves and tied this bit of string on to the door handle."

"Say," said Toddy, "you're pretty quick to work out how it happened."

"Whoever did this can get to hell off the place," said T. Burke, before Ponto could reply to Toddy's accusation. "A man could have been killed. And look at the mess! It'll take me all day to clean it up. I'm a pretty easy-going sort of bloke but I'm not standing for this sort of thing. It must have been one of you blokes—now who was it?"

"The same bastard who stuck the pole on the mantelpiece," said Ponto fiercely.

"I can see that. But who the hell was it? It must be one of you jokers," insisted T. Burke, "and whoever it was needs his head read."

"Well you can count me out for a start," said Sam, "I'm not loony and I never left my bed all night."

"That goes for me too," said Toddy.

T. Burke turned on Ponto. "Then it must have been this lazy

bastard," he snarled. "He's just hanging around to make trouble."

"Here now!" shouted Ponto. "You can cut that out. I didn't do it."

"Well, what are you going to do about it," shouted T. Burke. "One of you is a bloody liar, and that's flat." He paused thoughtfully. "And how the hell do I know you're not all in on it?"

"Look," said Sam reasonably, "whoever pulled these stunts is right off his rocker, but he must be cunning too. They've been worked out pretty carefully and there must be some reason for it. Are you sure you haven't got any enemies around here?"

"I've got one all right," said T. Burke, "and when I find out who it is there'll be a slight fuss, believe me!"

"Well, it wouldn't be any of us," Sam argued. "We've got nothing to gain by it."

"You just said whoever it was is crackers and cunning," said T. Burke. "He doesn't have to have a reason, in that case; but he'd better be ready for a quick trip if I catch him, that's all."

"Did anyone hear anything last night?" asked Sam.

"No, not a thing," said Toddy.

"Nor me," asserted Ponto.

"So nobody did it," said T. Burke. "All right, we'll forget about it—only I *won't* forget. The bastard who done this has only got to make one slip and I'll have 'im. I'll put the bastard up! That's what I'll do. And I won't be caught in any of your booby-traps so easy next time. Now we'll have to clear some of this mess out of the way so I can get at the stove."

They lifted the shelves back into place and tied the wire across them. Then Ponto, Toddy and Sam began sweeping up the broken plates and things while T. Burke lit the fire.

As the smoke billowed out round T. Burke there was a dull explosion and the room filled with ashes and smoking pieces of wood. T. Burke reeled back from the stove and they all stood silent in the smoky room. Sam kicked an ember on to the hearth.

"What was that?" asked Ponto.

"Looks as if one of you put one of these in the ashes of the fire," said T. Burke quietly, bending to pick up a split shotgun cartridge off the floor and holding it out for them to see.

Then there was another explosion and more ashes and embers were blown out around them. No one even ducked. They just stood there.

The phone in the passage rang short-short-long.

"Two of them," amended T. Burke, even more quietly. "What I said before still goes, only double. I'll thump the tripe out of whoever it is and then put him up!"

They swept all the embers on to the hearth and Sam re-lit the fire.

"It's lucky these weren't put away last night," said Ponto, indicating four plates on the bench, "otherwise we'd have nothing to eat off."

Toddy clearly remembered putting all the plates away the night before when he wiped the bench down but he didn't mention it to the others. There'd been enough scenes for one day.

During breakfast the others kept staring at Toddy until he could stand it no longer.

"What are you all staring at?" he burst out suddenly.

"You've forgotten to put your coat on," said Sam.

Toddy was so uncomfortable he couldn't concentrate on the meal and scuttled off to get his oilskin as soon as he'd finished his second chop.

They began the job of cleaning up. Sam sorted the broken from the unbroken. T. Burke went through it again, putting aside the things he thought he could fix. Toddy put the unfixable stuff in a box to take away and throw over the bank, while Ponto wandered back and forth with the clock, looking for somewhere to put it.

"Hey!" yelped Toddy from the porch. "Who done this?"

T. Burke, Ponto and Sam crowded into the porch doorway and found Toddy with his foot half in one of his gumboots. A neat job had been made of cutting eyes, nose and mouth out of the toe of each boot.

"Hell's bells," said T. Burke.

"Are you sure they're yours?" asked Sam.

"Course they are, I'd know them a mile off!"

"So would I," chuckled Ponto.

"This isn't funny, Ponto," said Toddy. He was so indignant his oilskin crackled.

"Someone seems to think it's funny," said T. Burke, looking at Ponto, who suddenly stopped grinning.

"They've got a rotten sense of humour, whoever it is," said Sam sympathetically. "We'll get you a new pair of boots as soon as we can, Toddy. In the meantime I'm afraid you're a sitter for a pair of wet feet every time you go out."

T. Burke shook his head hopelessly and went back to clearing a path through the debris with an old shovel. "Crazy," he muttered. "What the hell next!"

It took them the rest of the morning to tidy up the room. By the time they'd carted out the broken and useless stuff and stacked the rest neatly back on the shelves, half of them were empty.

After lunch they waited on the sledge for about half an hour while T. Burke got his tractor unflooded. Then he drove out, turned round in the paddock, back through the shed and two hundred yards down to the gate to pick up a medium-sized cardboard box of groceries that had been sitting there for two days.

Ponto and Toddy picked up the box and the bottom of it, soggy from the damp stand, gave way and spilled everything on to the ground.

"I'll have to go back to the house for another box," said T. Burke.

He took Sam with him to help load the empty box on to

the sledge and returned half an hour later. They put the stores into the new box and returned to the house. While T. Burke and Toddy put the tractor away Sam and Ponto stoked up the fire and put a mutton roast in the oven for tea.

During tea the phone in the passage rang three shorts and a long and T. Burke got up to answer it. He lifted the receiver, listened for a moment, said "No," and hung up.

"Wrong number," he said, sitting down to the table again.

After tea, T. Burke rummaged in the porch and came back into the kitchen with a gumboot, which he put on the table in front of Toddy.

"Here y'are. That doesn't leak. It'll keep one of your feet dry. The other boot's had it though. Young bloke I had workin' here got his foot under the discs. He left that behind when they took him into hospital and never came back for it."

Toddy looked at the gumboot for a few moments as though it still had a foot in it and then put it on the floor beside his chair.

"Thanks," he said. "I'll try it on in the morning."

"Hope it fits you," said Sam. "I've seen some trouble caused by crook boots in my time. There's been blokes tripped up, hooked up, hung up, chopped up, crippled, and God knows what because of bad boots. That's one thing I'm fussy about, a decent pair of clod-hoppers. I once saw a bloke get killed with a boot that didn't fit properly."

"They can trip you up all right," agreed T. Burke, whose own boots were as ill-fitting as any Sam had seen.

"This bloke didn't trip," said Sam. "In fact he wasn't even wearing the boots. His mate was."

"How did that come about?" asked Toddy.

"Well this bloke, Bill Duncan was his name, had been in town on the grog with his mate and they'd bought themselves a new pair of hob-nailed boots each when they were tight. Didn't even try them on. When they got back to the station they were shepherding on, they tried out these new boots and

Bill's fitted all right but his mate's were too big in the feet and too small round the top. He must have had a crook set of feet on him or something. Anyhow he wore them with the laces undone because he'd thrown his old ones away.

"They had a big mob of ewes to dip the next day and out they went, hangovers and all, to muster in these sheep. They got them into the yards all right but what with the dust and the heat the sheep got a bit lazy on it towards the middle of the afternoon. Bill and his mate had to pick up each sheep and dump it personally into the dip.

"A man with a hangover doesn't usually appreciate that sort of slogging and it wasn't long before they started taking it out on the dogs. Then Bill's mate let fly a kick at one of the dogs and missed. His boot flew off and caught Bill fair behind the ear. Knocked 'im cold. Bill was bending over the dip at the time and of course in he goes. His mate didn't see what had happened because he was still throwing everything he could lay his hands on at the dog.

"There was another bloke there who saw it but nobody took any notice of the bit of extra shouting he was doing. By the time he'd pushed his way through the yardful of sheep to where Bill was it was too late. Bill had hit the trail to the boneyard."

"I bet his mate was miserable about it," said Toddy.

"Not on your life," said Sam. "Couple of weeks later he'd awarded himself a medal from the Royal Humane Society. Had it worked out that Bill had slipped and had caught hold of the boot to save himself. When the boot and Bill disappeared in the dip, the mate said he fished out three sheep and the boot before he got old Bill."

"The rotten sod," said Toddy.

"Yes," said Sam, "proper mongrel of a bloke he turned out to be. There was a rumour that he used to blackmail an old aunt of his who hadn't paid her radio licence fee for years. He had her bluffed that they'd slap her in jail if they found out about it. Took her for hundreds before she worried herself to death over it."

"A bloke like that wouldn't last long in these parts," said T. Burke.

"Don't you believe it," said Sam. "He married himself into a dirty big estate up Nelson way a year or two later and made a fortune out of it. He's the mayor of Matarua now—not fifty miles from here. Just goes to show what you can get away with if you've got the hide."

"I'm going to bed," said T. Burke. "If I hear anyone sneakin' around in the night, look out. I'll be waiting for them."

"So will I," said Sam.

"Me too," said Toddy.

"I'll be going straight to sleep," said Ponto. "I've got nothing to worry about."

"You will have if it's your turn next," said T. Burke, going out into the passage. "Good night."

"Can you blame him?" said Sam. "It's a wonder he didn't boot us all out on the spot."

"He took it pretty calm all right," said Ponto. "Anyone else would have called the cops."

"He thinks it's one of us," said Toddy.

"It must be one of us," said Sam. "It couldn't possibly be anyone else."

Pay Sam and Ponto

Toddy lay awake waiting for T. Burke to get up. He'd wanted to go outside shortly after going to bed the night before but wasn't game to. He'd spent a very uncomfortable night and was deciding whether or not to get up and light the fire himself when he heard T. Burke's bedroom door open. He came so slowly up the passage the floor hardly creaked. Toddy heard him hesitate by the door into the kitchen and begin to come back along the passage.

Suddenly the phone shrilled two longs just beside him and he started so violently that he bumped against the wall.

"What was that?" demanded Ponto, waking suddenly. "What's wrong?"

"Should anything be?" called T. Burke sulkily through the wall.

"Thought I heard something," said Ponto.

"You'll hear plenty if I run into any of your bloody traps," said T. Burke.

"You needn't start calling them my bloody traps," said Ponto.

"Ar, we're all getting nervous," said Sam, getting out of bed. "Hold on, Burky. I'll give you a hand with the fire. You've been getting up first every morning."

He went out into the kitchen where T. Burke was poking suspiciously in the ashes of the stove with a piece of stick.

"I don't think we'll have any more of that kind of trouble," he said confidently. "Whichever one of them it was knows we're on the lookout for him."

T. Burke continued sifting through the ashes with his bit of wood.

"I'm not taking any chances," he said. "I just hope whoever it was has another go. They won't get away with it again."

"I'll tell you what I think," said Sam quietly—but then he heard Toddy coming up the passage and didn't tell T. Burke what he thought after all.

They spent all morning talking about getting a sledge-load of totara for firewood and then set out to do it.

T. Burke started his tractor in record time and they piled on to the sledge behind him and braced themselves for one of T. Burke's flying take-offs. But they weren't prepared for what happened after that. They'd hardly travelled ten feet when there was a splintering, rending crash behind them and the tractor was dragged to a stop quicker than T. Burke could ever have done it. Toddy, Ponto and Sam landed in a sprawling heap in the mud between the tractor and the sledge.

"What the hell was that?" yelled T. Burke, climbing off the tractor.

His three muddy workers picked themselves up and stood looking at the wreckage. It was obvious what had happened. Someone had tied the tractor to the back of the shed with a doubled length of fencing-wire, which must have been buried in the mud. It wasn't exactly what you'd call a young building and the whole corner had been torn out of it. The roof at that end sagged halfway to the ground.

They looked at each other completely staggered for a few moments and then Ponto said: "Who done that?"

"I don't know who done it," said T. Burke, "but that shed was built by my old dad and you had no right to wreck it. What the hell's the point of all these useless tricks? The next time anything happens the lot of you can get off the place."

They untied the wire and T. Burke started his tractor. The others got on to the sledge without speaking. They'd slithered along the track for several hundred yards when Toddy turned to Ponto and said: "Can you smell anything?"

"Yeah, you," said Ponto sulkily.

"Something's burning," insisted Toddy. "The tractor might

be catching on fire."

"They always stink a bit when they warm up," explained Sam. "Probably a bit of oil spilt on the exhaust."

But before they'd gone very much further choking fumes and smoke came billowing out round the tractor. T. Burke stopped the motor and jumped off.

"What the hell next!" he shouted.

Sam and Toddy stepped clear of the smoke and Ponto panicked.

"Look out!" he yelled diving off the sledge and running stiffly, like an old man, through the mud. "We're going to be blown up with petrol!"

Sam ignored him and peered through the smoke at the motor.

"What's burning?" asked T. Burke.

"This," said Sam, holding up a few soft blobs of candle-grease, held together by the wicks. "It's melted all over the manifold. No wonder she pongs a bit."

"How did a candle get in there?" asked Toddy.

"I'll give you three guesses," said T. Burke heavily. "One of you bastards put it there."

"We'll have to clean it off before we can go any further," said Sam.

T. Burke turned from watching Ponto's slow return. "You're not going any further," he said. "You can hit the track first thing in the morning. The whole lousy bunch of you!"

No one could think of anything to say. The tractor stood with faint trails of smoke wafting around it. Sam stood looking thoughtful. T. Burke stood looking at his tractor. Ponto came up looking bewildered and Toddy shuffled in the mud with his good gumboot, looking ridiculous.

At last Sam spoke.

"That's fair enough, Burky. I don't blame you in the least. I'd do the same myself. We'll give you a hand to clean up the tractor and get that load of wood."

"I don't know that a man can trust you to give him a hand,"

muttered T. Burke dubiously, but he let Sam clean all the grease off the tractor and they all helped to load the wood.

It began to rain while they were unloading the sledge so they went inside to get a meal ready. After tea T. Burke took down one of the lamps and said: "I know you blokes are broke and you don't deserve any pay, after all the damage you've done round the place, but I'll give you a tenner to get you out of the district."

"We'll just borrow it off you, Burky," said Sam. "I'll post it back to you as soon as I get on my feet again."

"Please yourself about that," said T. Burke. "But it'll be worth a tenner to get rid of you." And he went off to bed without another word.

As soon as he'd gone Toddy said excitedly to Ponto and Sam:

"I've got an idea who it is!"

"Who it is?" said Ponto.

"Who's been playing those tricks."

"Who then?"

"It's not one of us at all. It's someone who's been here all the time!"

"What, Burky?"

"No. His wife!"

"His wife?"

There was a silence while Ponto and Sam thought about it.

"No," decided Sam at last. "If there was anyone hanging around here we'd be bound to catch on."

"But what if he keeps her hidden in his bedroom or in the old woolshed?" insisted Toddy

"Ar, you've been reading too many books," scoffed Ponto. "You can't take a step in this place without everyone hearing."

"Someone can," Sam reminded him. "But all the same, I don't think Toddy's on the right track. It's not a woman's caper. Those rigs were simple enough but they were bloody clever. I don't care what you say."

"A woman can be clever too," said Toddy in defence of his theory.

"No show," said Ponto finally. "You'd never catch a woman smashing up her own gear like that. Besides, we all know bloody well there's just T. Burke and ourselves."

"What about that publican from down the road?" said Toddy suddenly. "He's lousy enough to have a go at anything."

"With his weight he'd go right through this floor, let alone walk around quietly on it," said Sam. "Anyway—what would he gain by it?"

"What would anyone gain by it?"

"Nope. We're back where we started," said Ponto, reaching for the lamp. "It's either one of us or T. Burke."

He led the way up the passage to their bedroom.

Some time in the early hours of the morning Sam was awakened by Toddy, who was leaning over with one hand on the floor to shake him gently.

"Hey, Sam, Sam, it's raining."

"What's the matter, can't you sleep?"

"It's raining. We won't be able to go tomorrow."

"Go to sleep."

Toddy leaned back into his bed and Sam rolled over to go back to sleep. Then Toddy was shaking him again, more urgently this time.

"Wake up. Listen!" he was whispering. "What's that noise out there?"

Sam woke up and listened. There was only the sound of light rain on the roof and the irregular rattle of a loose sheet of roofing iron.

"Can't hear a thing," whispered Sam, so as not to wake Ponto.

"I heard someone splashing."

"What sort of splashing?"

"Like pouring water or something."

"Probably a hole in the roof."

"No—listen!"

And Sam heard a rhythmic splashing of water coming faintly from somewhere beyond the passage. He and Toddy lay listening in the dark, doing more wondering than breathing.

"Wake up Ponto," decided Sam after a few minutes, during which time the noise had become louder. "You're the nearest."

Toddy rustled across to shake Ponto, who awoke grunting like a pig in a wallow.

"What's wrong?" he mumbled thickly. "What's the bloody idea? It's not even daylight yet!"

"Shh," hissed Toddy, "someone's splashing!"

"Good on them. Leave 'em to it," said Ponto. Then he propped himself up on one elbow.

"Someone's what?"

"Don't make a sound. We heard someone splashing water round."

"Did you? What was it? You awake, Sam?"

"Yeah—listen!"

They listened to the noise in silence for a few moments. The splashing could be distinctly heard above the sound of the rain on the roof.

"Hear that?" asked Toddy.

"Yeah," whispered Sam, slowly swinging his feet out of bed. "Let's go and have a look."

"No!" said Ponto quickly. "It mightn't be safe."

"If it's someone rigging another trap they won't be safe," whispered Sam grimly. "Light the lamp, Toddy. I'm going to see what's going on out there."

Toddy lit the lamp and Sam creaked across the floor in his socks, took it from him and crept to the door.

"Be a beaut if he catches Burky up to something," whispered Ponto enthusiastically to Toddy, at the same time making it plain that he had no intention of getting out of bed to help.

Sam opened the door quickly and the phone up the passage

fell to the floor with a loud ringing bang, followed by Sam's lamp, which lay there hissing and unbroken. Ponto clutched a fistful of blankets nervously at his chin and Toddy was out of bed and beside Sam in time to pick up the lamp first. The dinging of the phone bell died in the noise of rain and T. Burke getting up.

"Was that the phone?" asked Toddy, peering up the passage.

"Who's that?" called Sam. "You there, Burky?"

T. Burke's bedroom door scraped open behind them.

"What's up?" he called uncertainly.

"We don't know," replied Sam. "Sounds as if the phone's fallen." He moved slowly forward, holding the lamp out in front of him, followed by T. Burke, Toddy and Ponto in that order, until he could see where the phone lay on the floor.

"She's fallen all right," said Sam.

"And what's this rope for?" asked T. Burke heavily.

And they saw that a piece of twine was tied to the phone. It ran up over the nail in the wall on which the phone-book usually hung above the phone. The nail had been doubled over to act as a pulley for the twine, the free end of which lay loosely on the floor.

"It's another of those rig-ups," said Sam, in answer to T. Burke's query. "As soon as I opened the door—bang, down she comes."

"And now you've busted me bloody phone," said T. Burke. "Is there anything else you'd like to get stuck into while you're on the job? Me floor hasn't been ripped up yet."

"I didn't touch your phone," said Sam. "As I said, I just opened the bedroom door and there was this crash. Let's have a look at the rope. That must have something to do with it."

He picked up the loose end of the twine and stretched it up the passage.

"See here," he said. "See how the end of this rope's doubled and squashed flat?" He held the rope-end near the lamp Toddy was holding so they could examine it closely.

"Someone's tied the rope on to the phone, run it up through

that nail and up the passage here to our bedroom door. They've jammed it in the door to take the weight and then unscrewed the phone and cut the wires. When I opened the door it released the rope and bingo!"

"And just what were you doing out here at this time of the morning?" asked T. Burke.

"We heard water splashing and thought the roof must have sprung a leak," explained Toddy. "Sam was just going to have a look!"

"Hey," said Ponto, "I can still hear it—listen!"

They listened.

"It's in the kitchen," said Sam. "Bring the lamp, Toddy."

"If you open that door the whole bloody roof'll probably cave in on us," said T. Burke.

Sam stopped with his hand on the kitchen door. He looked quietly from Toddy to Ponto and then to T. Burke.

"Shall I open it?" he asked.

"Sure," said T. Burke. "Go ahead and open it. I can't wait to see you get caught in one of your own traps."

Sam ignored the remark and slowly turned the door-handle. Nothing happened. He gently pushed the door open a few inches. No crash. He peeped into the kitchen. It was just light.

"What is it this time?" asked T. Burke.

"What's the splashing?" asked Ponto.

"Far as I can make out someone's bent the guttering in through the window and water off the roof is running on to the table," replied Sam. "There's water everywhere. Have a look."

They looked in turn through the partly-open door at what Sam had described. None of them could make any more of it than Sam had and they all agreed that they'd better take it carefully.

"Someone had better go round to the back door, and have a look through the window," said Sam. "Can you get out the front door?" he asked T. Burke.

"No, it's nailed up. Hinges are gone."

"Well I'll climb out one of the windows," said Sam.

He went up the passage and into one of the spare rooms, where he lifted one of the windows easily out of its frame and climbed out. It was just getting daylight. He ran through the rain to the back door, opened it and walked into the kitchen.

"It's okay," he called to the others. "There's just this spouting arrangement in here."

T. Burke led Toddy and Ponto into the room. A piece of spouting had been torn loose and poked in the window, which was open a few inches at the top. Water from the roof had been running on to the table and out through gaps in the floor-boards. The splashing had saturated floor, walls and furniture and the room had the damp chill of a sunless corner of the rain-forest. Sam shivered like a wet dog shaking.

"Now this," said T. Burke, looking at the mess. "Another little prank, eh! Well, it'll be the last chance you get."

He set about lighting the fire, after carefully examining the stove, the wood, the axe, and the pots. After breakfast he fetched a ragged cheque-book, scratch-point pen and a big bottle of ink from his bedroom and set them up on a dry corner of the table. It took him several minutes to write out the cheque. He handed it to Sam. It read:

PAY Sam and Ponto.

THE SUM OF Ten quid

SIGNED   T. Burke.

He turned to Toddy. "I don't think you've had anything to do with what's been going on, Toddy," he said. "You can stay here if you like. I need an active bloke to help out round the place. Got to get it fenced off so I can winter more stock. Plenty to do before the lambing starts. Then there'll be docking and shearing—what about it?"

"Well, thanks all the same . . ." began Toddy. He stopped and looked at Ponto and Sam.

"A good idea," said Sam. "You stay on, Toddy. I know you like it here. The job was just made for you." Then, seeing that

Toddy was still undecided, he added: "It'll be easier for Ponto and me to get a job if there's only two of us. Three's always a bit hard to place—isn't that so, Ponto?"

"Yeah," said Ponto disinterestedly.

So Toddy stayed, and Ponto and Sam went off down T. Burke's wet, winding drive. Toddy watched them stop at the gate to turn their collars up and then head north up the main road. Then he went back into the warm old kitchen, where T. Burke sat with his feet in the oven, and began thinking up a poem about Sam and Ponto.

Heading North

SAM AND PONTO were walking along in silence. Ponto, two chains behind, was sulking because Sam hadn't agreed that they should stop for a beer at the pub where they'd been fleeced on their way south. And Sam was brooding about having to go back over a road he'd so recently travelled. It had stopped raining but there was no likelihood of their seeing anything of the sun that day, or for quite a few days to come, the way the weather had been.

Sam came to a country store and waited for Ponto to catch up.

"We might try cashing that cheque of Burky's here," he suggested.

Ponto grunted his agreement and they went into the store. The elderly storekeeper glanced at the cheque and gave them the cash as though he got them like that every day. They bought biscuits and tobacco and went back on to the road in case they missed a lift.

"Rum go at T. Burke's there," said Ponto, after he'd eaten most of the biscuits and rolled himself a smoke.

"Yeah," said Sam.

"Wasn't you, was it?" asked Ponto.

"No, it wasn't me."

"Must've been Toddy. Queer that, you wouldn't think he was the sort of a bloke."

"It wasn't Toddy," said Sam.

"In that case it must have been you, because I know it wasn't me."

"It was Burky himself," said Sam quietly. "I'm sure of it."

"Come off it! He'd be crazy."

"He must be," said Sam. "The way I figure it he's the only one who could have done it."

"How do you work that one out?"

"Well, for a start, none of us could have sneaked in and out of the room without risking waking the others up. That had me thinking at first and when it went on happening I was pretty certain it must be someone else."

"Could be," said Ponto noncommittally.

"Then there was the rope," continued Sam. "I didn't see any rope like that used on the phone till I went through one of the spare rooms to get out the window. There was a roll of it in there and I don't think you and Toddy had ever been that far up the passage."

"Then I noticed that if you lift the back door as you open it there's hardly any noise, so I figured that whoever was getting in and out of the kitchen was using that way. The window in our room was nailed up and, as I say, none of us could have sneaked in and out safely anyway. Besides that, a bloke can't walk round in a place like Burky's without knowing it pretty well, in spite of the noise the wind and rain makes.

"Another thing, did you notice any candles lying around anywhere?"

"No. Come to think of it I didn't!" said Ponto. "There was just them two lamps."

"And we had a good chance to go through all the gear in the kitchen when we were cleaning up," said Sam. "Burky must have kept a few in his bedroom in case his lamp cut out on him."

"It's all only guessing," said Ponto. "I still reckon it could have been Toddy."

"No, it was Burky all right," said Sam. "Can you tie a running-bowline?"

"That's a kind of knot, isn't it?"

"Yeah, it was the knot Burky used to tie that load of wood on to the sledge with yesterday. And the same knot was used to tie the rope on to the phone in the passage last night. Another thing I noticed about that was how the hell could one of us jam the rope in our door when we were all inside the room?"

"That's a tricky one," said Ponto. "But it's not impossible."

"No, it's not impossible but you'd have to be lucky to get away with it."

"It looks a bit suspicious all right," admitted Ponto.

"There's one more thing that really convinced me it was Burky," added Sam.

"What's that?"

"The wire on the tractor. Every man who's done a bit of fencing has his own particular way of tying-off number-eight wire. Some leave it wound along the strain, some blokes double it half back, some double it right back and then over itself again, some take a couple of turns in it and some take a dozen, but I've never seen two men tie wire off in exactly the same way."

"But that doesn't mean Burky tied the wire on to the tractor."

"Too right it does. It was tied in the same way as Burky always does it. I'd noticed the way he did it when we were working on the sheep-yards. And it was the same as all the other bits of wire round the place."

"It certainly looks a bit like it was old Burky," said Ponto. "But what the hell was the idea of the whole caper?"

"Could be anything," said Sam. "We know that whoever it was, was as mad as a gum-digger's dog and shrewd at the same time. Burky looked a bit of a queer sod at times there but you wouldn't think he was all that loose. It might be that he's been living on his own too long. A bit bush-happy on it. One thing I'm sure of though, he didn't have it in for anyone in particular. They were just some sort of joke, done in the spirit of the occasion, you might say. I don't think they were planned in advance, either. Did you notice how Toddy's gumboots got the treatment the morning after I'd been telling you about the old roadman's gumboot?"

"Yeah, but then he goes and gives Toddy another boot. It doesn't add up."

"None of it does," agreed Sam. "I suppose one of those psychologist blokes could tell what's gone haywire with old Burky but it's way out of my line of country."

"What about Toddy?" asked Ponto suddenly. "Do you think he'll be all right?"

"Sure of it," said Sam. "Burky doesn't want to hurt anybody. He sprung most of those traps on himself. If he'd wanted anyone to get knocked around he could easily have let us cop it. And I think he's too crafty to pull anything with just himself and Toddy there. Besides Toddy would know straight away that it was him. He seemed genuine enough about wanting Toddy to stay there.

"I think the whole thing was just the result of Burky's sense of humour going cockeyed on him," concluded Sam. "He'll be okay with a bit of regular company. A good pair, him and Toddy."

"She's a queer outfit, all the same," said Ponto. And finding Sam's pace a bit demanding on his depleted reserves of energy, he began to fall behind a little.

They plodded on for another half-hour and then Sam stopped and held up his hand.

"Listen," he said. "I think I can hear a car coming."

"Yes," said Ponto. "I can hear it now."

"Sounds like a truck."

"It's going the wrong way."

"No, it's not, listen!"

"It's a tractor."

"No, it's going too fast for that."

"It's a bloody grader!"

"Here it comes!"

"It's a van. Hell, look at it!"

"Wave him down."

"Look out! He's going off the road!"

"No, he's right."

"He's stopping!"

And a great rattly old van slid to a swaying, shuddering stop that could only have been achieved by the gear-lever being rammed into reverse. The driver jumped out with a loud curse, which he threw at the world in general, and a big block of wood, which he threw behind a front wheel to prevent the contraption from running backwards down the slope.

"Bloody motor stalled," he said, kicking at the wheel. "I couldn't get her out of gear in time. Clutch is a bit crook."

This was Scrubby O'Leary. Six foot-odd tall by about six inches through and so skinny you'd think he'd bend off at the pockets in a strong wind. Long curly black hair, ordinary clothes, crook teeth, and the whole outfit covered with grease and oil. He'd spent the season white-baiting and stayed on in South Westland driving a bulldozer for the Ministry of Works He was heading north because he couldn't get any further south than he'd been. His van, which he'd won off a Maori in a poker game, used a gallon of oil every ten miles or so and was due to be topped up again from one of the four-gallon tins of waste oil he carried in the back.

All this Ponto and Sam learned in the time it took him to tell them. In the back of the vehicle, apart from the five tins of oil, were half a dozen worn-out tyres, a pile of tubes, levers, spanners, jacks, axes, boxes of nuts and bolts, ropes and just about everything else you can think of in the way of spare parts, from carburettors and coils to wheel-bearings and king-pins. Scrubby himself was almost as mechanical as his van. As well as smelling the same, his pockets were full of nuts, valves, spanners, pipe-fittings, cotter-pins, bits of wire and rag, and sundry other pieces of what the van was made of.

He poured about a gallon of dirty black oil into the motor and a pint or so into the petrol-tank.

"I like to stick a bit of oil in with the gas," he explained. "The oil-pump's a bit worn and me valves start stickin' if they get too dry." He swung an affectionate kick at a half-flat rear tyre. "Struth, we could use a bit of wind in this," he said. "Throw me out the pump—what did you say your name was, mate?"

"Sam," said Sam, handing him the required instrument.

"Thanks, Sam." And they took it in turns to work the pump until the rim of the wheel was safely clear of the road. Then Scrubby topped off the leaking radiator from another four-gallon tin and they were ready to move.

Getting the van started turned out to be an intricate and delicate business. Refusing Sam's offer of assistance on the grounds that "she was a temperamental old bitch", Scrubby joined three of a dozen loose wires hanging down behind the dashboard. Then he took off one of his boots and propped it against the accelerator for the right amount of revs. Then the choke had to be adjusted to the correct thousandth of an inch. Something to do with the distributor had to be done and then Scrubby inserted the crank-handle, poured a precise amount of petrol into the carburettor from a bottle on the floor of the cab and dashed round to wind furiously on the crank-handle. After a hundred turns the motor spat raggedly for a few minutes, gave up the unequal struggle and roared dangerously into life. Scrubby dropped the bonnet into place, threw the crank-handle into the cab and put his other boot back on, keeping the motor running at a good shuddering speed by holding his hand on the accelerator. They all climbed in.

Scrubby dragged the machine into gear and forced it out into the road. He soon had it lumbering along at a pace that defied almost every mechanical principle that had gone into its manufacture.

By bullying the van into maintaining a tortured thirty-five miles an hour, it was still early afternoon when they ran out of petrol eight miles short of Hokitika.

"Nothing to worry about," said Scrubby. "It's just that the petrol-pipe doesn't reach right into the bottom of the tank.

There's still a bit of gas in her. We'll siphon some out and run it straight into the carb. out of the tin."

He emptied one of the oil-tins into the motor and siphoned it half-full of petrol with the windscreen-wiper-hose.

And they arrived in Hokitika with Sam sitting on the one good mudguard, holding the tin of petrol and drip-feeding Scrubby's carburettor.

Then they found Scrubby's weakness. He was terrified of traffic cops. They only stayed in the town long enough to service the van and themselves and lit out for somewhere quieter.

The Last Drink

THE SHORT WINTER DAY was dying on the mountain tops, several thousand feet above them. The van was graunching its way deafeningly up a gentle slope in second gear and Sam was having trouble rolling a smoke because of the bouncing and swaying.

"Have to stop soon," shouted Scrubby, at the top of his voice in Ponto's ear.

"What?"

"Have to stop soon," roared Scrubby. "We've got no lights!"

Ponto nodded uncomprehendingly and Scrubby grinned across at Sam. He was always grinning, which made it a bit rough on the eyesight because of his bad teeth. He didn't even stop grinning when they nearly went off the road, which was often enough. Something to do with the tie-rods.

It began to get really dark but in several miles there hadn't been one place on the narrow road where they could safely pull over to the side. Scrubby stopped grinning as visibility shortened and even Sam began to look a little disturbed.

Suddenly they made out the lights of a building up ahead. It was a pub. Scrubby shouted something unintelligible and went into his pulling-up routine. He chopped her down through the gears; third, second, low and then a sudden, grating shove and the trembling vehicle was in reverse and shrieking to a shuddering stop outside the pub. Sam and Ponto climbed out and walked stiffly back and forth in the deafening silence while Scrubby did something under the bonnet of his hissing van.

"Should be in Marlborough by this time tomorrow," observed Sam.

"But we'll have to stay here for tonight," said Ponto contentedly.

"Yeah, we'll book ourselves in," said Scrubby, joining them. "We can knock a few beers back after we've had something to eat." He was talking Ponto's language.

"I can give you a feed," said the publican, "but I've only got one room with a double bed to offer you."

"You pretty full up?" asked Sam.

"No, that's the only room I've got ready. The missus doesn't reckon it's worth keeping the others going. We don't get many people staying the night here. It's only an hour's run into town."

"Not for us," grinned Scrubby. "We could all fit in a double bed, couldn't we?" he asked, turning to Sam and Ponto.

"Yeah, easy," said Sam.

"Room four, straight up the passage," said the publican. And that was settled.

After a meal of mutton stew and steam pudding Ponto retired to the bar while Scrubby and Sam went to look for a bathroom, which they found after trying every other door in the passage.

"What's the score on your mate, Sam?" asked Scrubby, blowing noisily through a face-full of soapy water.

"Just a bloke I teamed up with a few weeks back," replied Sam, running the publican's razor down the side of his face. "If he was as fond of work as he is of grog he'd be a hard man to beat. He's not very bright as a matter of fact. Real dumb at times. And he's got absolutely no sense of humour," he added, as though that summed up Ponto completely.

They joined Ponto at the bar. He had already got into his stride and drank a schooner to each of Scrubby's and Sam's eight-ounce beers. The only others in the bar were a roadman and his wife drinking whisky in the far corner, and the publican, who was drinking with everybody.

After a half-hour of drinking and chatting Ponto asked: "Where is it?"

"You'll have to use the inside one," said the publican apologetically. "We had a bit of an accident with the one outside. Second door on the left up the passage."

"What happened to it?" asked Sam, when Ponto had gone off.

"A bloke who was through here three or four weeks back reckoned he could blow the bottom of the hole bigger with gelignite so it'd drain better, but he must have used about ten plugs. Blew the whole box'n dice to bits. The old place is temporarily out of order till I get round to building another. I suppose I should have taken it out of that joker's hide, but he was a pretty big bloke."

"Stiff luck," said Sam sympathetically.

"Tough all right," said Scrubby. "What was his name?"

"Harvey Wilson," said the publican.

"Do you think it'll rain again?" asked Sam.

Just then Ponto returned and sank three-quarters of his schooner in one smooth movement.

"That's better," he said. "Have one with me, chief."

"Don't mind if I do," said the publican, filling the glasses. "If they were all like you a publican's life would be much happier."

"And if publicans were all like Ponto they'd be dead inside three months," laughed Sam.

"That'll be four and three, thanks," said the publican to Ponto.

Ponto dug unsuccessfully into his pockets. "You'll have to give me some more money," he said to Sam. "I'm swept again."

"Yeah, sure," said Sam. "Tell you what, we'll split up what we've got left between us—are you holding okay, Scrubby?"

"Yeah, I've got plenty, thanks," said Scrubby.

Sam counted all the money out of his pockets on to the bar and announced a total of "Eight pound fifteen and six. How much each does that work out at?"

Ponto dipped a finger in his beer and wrote on the bar: "Four into eight goes one and carry four . . ."

They all began to laugh. "You get four pound seven and ninepence each," chuckled the publican. "And you can have this one on the house."

At half-past three in the morning Scrubby, Sam, the publican, and even Ponto had had quite enough to drink. The publican herded them in the direction of their bedroom.

"Don't make any noise," he shouted after them in a whisper. "If the missus wakes up there'll be murder done!"

They found the room and sat on the edge of the bed, having trouble getting their bootlaces undone. Scrubby's accelerator boot had been unlaced all the time. He looked at it for a few moments and then began to lace it up. Sam got him straightened out on the matter and they clambered into bed. Sam got between the sheets, Scrubby got between the top sheet and the first blanket and Ponto sorted out a nest for himself between the first and second blankets, right on the edge of the bed. He wasn't going to take his filthy jacket off but Sam hissed such indignant objections that he at last threw the offending garment on the floor and pulled the blankets over his head.

"Last into bed has to turn the light out," said Sam.

"Yeah," mumbled Scrubby. "Turn the bloody light out."

So Ponto had to get up again, cursing his mates as though they were women drivers.

Sam and Ponto were woken next morning by Scrubby crawling across them to get up. Too early. Far too early. They followed each other blearily out into a patch of freezing sunlight by the van. The pub was silent and still. Ponto sat himself gently on the running-board.

"Never again," he croaked. "I'm giving up the booze. It's not worth it. It's all right when you're young but when a man gets up around my age he can't take it any more. Too tough on 'im."

"Eh?" said Sam, who was leaning on a mudguard staring

vacantly at Scrubby, who was leaning on the other mudguard staring back.

"What's the time?" croaked Ponto.

Scrubby squinted at his watch. "Twenty past seven," he groaned. And they lapsed into silence.

A crooked arm of smoke despumated wearily from the hotel chimney and flexed its fingers in the still air over their heads. None of them saw it.

A window went up in the hotel. "Hey," called the publican cheerfully. "Do you blokes feel like a feed of porridge and bacon?"

Sam shook his head, Scrubby winced, and Ponto gurgled and rumbled.

After a while Scrubby whispered hoarsely, "I suppose we'd better get goin'."

"Yeah," croaked Sam.

Neither of them moved.

"Want a shove?" asked Sam after another spell of silent contemplation.

"We'd never shift her," groaned Scrubby. "Have to crank the old bitch. Should have parked her on a hill."

"Where's the handle?"

"On the floor of the cab."

"Shall I get it?"

"Yeah."

Sam pushed himself away from the mudguard and got Scrubby's crank-handle out of the cab. When he slammed the door Ponto nearly fell off the opposite running-board.

"How about going and paying our respects and our bill?" said Sam to Ponto, handing him a couple of crumpled pound-notes.

Ponto was too weak to argue. He lurched to his feet, took the money and shambled across to the pub.

Scrubby prepared the van for starting.

"You wind 'er up and I'll work the choke," he whispered hoarsely to Sam, climbing carefully into the driver's seat.

171

Sam wound weakly for about five minutes before the motor blundered into action with such an alarming, grinding roar that he hopped in beside Ponto before something blew up.

They rattled away from the horrible little pub swearing never again to touch the grog.

"Except maybe one beer to put us right after last night," amended Ponto, who was beginning to feel a little better.

One of Us

BECAUSE OF HIS FEAR OF TRAFFIC COPS, Scrubby detoured every little town along the road that he came to. And the places he had to pass through made him so nervous that any traffic cop would have noticed him straight away. However they'd got well along the road towards Blenheim without any trouble from that quarter. They'd been hoping to find a pub before dark but this time it looked as though they were beaten. Scrubby pulled into a picnic area among some trees and stopped the motor.

"Oil stop," he said. "I can hear the big-ends rattling again."

"Doesn't look like we'll get much further today," said Sam.

"No, we might as well bunk down here for the night," agreed Scrubby. "I've got a blanket or two and a few sacks. Is there any of that bread and cheese left, Ponto?"

"Yeah," said Ponto round a mouthful of it.

"Sounds like our best move," said Sam. "I think I'll throw a bit of this wood in a heap and light a fire. Highway Hotel, cheese on toast for dinnah!"

Sam and Ponto gathered armfuls of wood and Sam built up a fire, which he drenched in oil from one of Scrubby's tins and lit. Scrubby threw four dirty grey blankets (with patches cut out where the hotel or hospital names had been printed) and a heap of oily sacks out of the van. By the time they were comfortably seated on the blankets round the fire it was properly dark.

"Where do you think we are?" asked Sam, scraping at a piece of burnt toast with the axe-head they were using for a bread-knife.

"We should make Blenheim by tomorrow night, and be back in Reefton a day or two after," said Scrubby.

"What's the hurry?" asked Ponto.

"I've got a lot of gear in Blenheim. I'll sell what I can and get myself a smaller bomb," said Scrubby. "This old girl gets a bit too thirsty on a long trip and I want to go down south for next summer. They tell me there's a lot of dough to be picked up diving for paua-shell. I'd like to have a go at it."

"What's the attraction in Reefton?" asked Sam.

"I think I can get a small contract cutting white-pine mine props," explained Scrubby. "I wouldn't mind a mate on it, actually. Are any of you blokes interested? It's bloody hard work but the money's good."

"I don't think I'd go for it much," said Ponto truthfully. "I prefer working on my own," he added, untruthfully.

"I'd like to tackle it," said Sam. "But what are you going to do, Ponto?"

"I'll think of something," said Ponto. And he did. In the morning he was gone.

"Where's Ponto?" asked Scrubby, sitting up yawning among his heap of sacks and blankets.

"Oh, he'll be around somewhere," said Sam, standing and stretching. But Ponto was around nowhere.

"He's a queer bird, that," said Scrubby. "Wonder where he is?"

"I think all that talk about hard work and money last night scared the pants off him," said Sam. "He doesn't think much of either of them."

"Can't say I'm very sorry to lose him," said Scrubby. "What made you hang around with him in the first place?"

"He lent me a fiver when I was broke," said Sam simply. "I didn't get a chance to pay it back—can you see my boots anywhere?"

"No," said Scrubby, looking around. "Where's mine?"

"That's funny, they were sitting right by this wheel here." They found their boots. Hanging in a tree above the van by a piece of number-eight wire. Sam had a look at the way the wire was tied and began to laugh.

He laughed the kind of laugh you only hear once every few years. A helpless, staggering, knee-slapping, back-thumping, side-of-van pounding, weeping, coughing, doubled-up laugh that went on for several minutes.

"Ponto . . . Ponto . . . Ponto . . .," the name came in gulps between gusts of laughter. And then, regaining control of his voice, "You lousy, lazy, loafing, useless, rotten, lowdown bastard. You . . ." And so on.

Scrubby just looked.

"Scrubby, old boy, I'll tell you a yarn that'll curl your back teeth!" said Sam, his voice a mixture of appreciation and exasperation. "A yarn about a bloke who's not very bright, real dumb in fact, and who's got absolutely no sense of humour whatever!"

"The first thing I noticed about Ponto was that he hated the idea of getting a job, he'd rather bludge, but I didn't realise how work-shy he was until we got a job on a farm down the Coast. Every time we got some work lined up something drastic would happen to hold up the job."

"Drastic? Like what?"

"Like the whole kitchen cupboard rigged up to crash down when we opened the door. Stuff set up in the night like booby-traps. I tell you, it was pretty weird. There were only me and Ponto and a bloke called Toddy we'd picked up along the way, and the old bloke we were working for. And someone was going to a hell of a lot of trouble to sabotage our jobs. It was only a matter of time before we got kicked off the place. I didn't know Ponto or Toddy very well. I even suspected the boss at one stage, but that didn't make sense either. In fact he was more hacked-off than I was, and you couldn't blame him. He'd given us a job and one of us immediately starts wrecking his place. They smashed all the stuff on his mantelpiece, and believe me there was a fair bit of it. They broke all his crockery and a lot of other gear, they blew up his stove with shotgun cartridges and ran water off the roof all over his kitchen."

"Hell's bells!" said Scrubby. "Someone sure didn't want that job all right!"

"Yeah, well I knew that one more stunt like that and we were down the road, and we were broke. It's easy enough to see looking back on it, but at the time the only one I knew was innocent was me, so I decided to rig up a little caper of my own and watch the others when they sprung it, to see if I could trick whoever it was into giving themselves away."

"What did you do?"

"We were all going off on the tractor the next day so I snuck out while they were cooking tea and tied the tractor onto the shed with some fencing wire and covered it with mud and hay and stuff. It worked a bit better than I intended, dragged the whole end out of the poor bloke's shed when we took off. I watched how the others took it but there wasn't a clue. They were all just surprised. And not only that, our prankster had gone and stuck a blasted candle on the manifold of the tractor. Stunk us off the job."

Scrubby nodded. "But you must have seen what an odd-ball Ponto was by this time."

"Oh you could see he was an odd-ball all right, but our other mate Toddy was a gold-plated odd-ball in his own right. And the bloke we were supposed to be working for was a professional odd-ball as well. In fact we were the oddest bunch of balls you'd ever want to run into. And one of us was deliberately trying to bring us all undone."

"What happened in the finish?"

"He won, and got away with it — this time. The boss gave me and Ponto a tenner and told us to git. He never believed it was Toddy who done all that, and he was right. Him and Toddy were kind of kindred souls, they'll be getting along great guns. If I'm ever back down that way I'll call in and let 'em know about Ponto. I don't like the idea of being suspected of being that lazy and ratbaggish."

"Don't blame you," said Scrubby. "When did you actually realise it was Ponto?"

"I wasn't certain until I saw how he tied that wire on our boots. I taught him how to tie wire like that, I don't think he'd ever done it before. It's his way of telling me it was him."

"What'll you do if you ever run into him again?"

"Nothin', he's in enough trouble as it is. The poor coot's going to run into strife wherever he goes."

"Sure sounds like he's slipped a cog somewhere along the way. What do you think's actually wrong with him?"

"His backside's too hungry for the ground," said Sam, "and he's got a lousy sense of humour. Now let's get this heap of yours cranked-up, Scrubby. There's a brand-new adventure waiting for us on the other side of the hill."

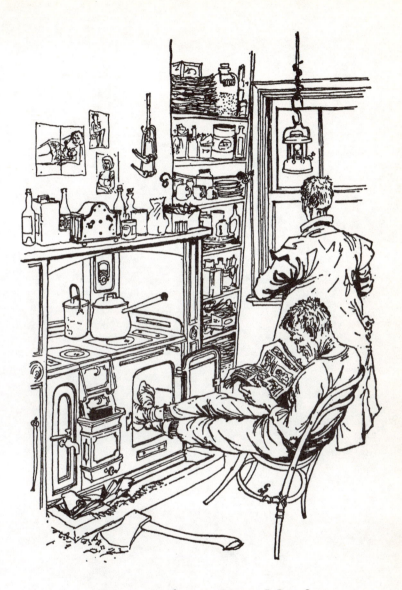

Got a Light on You, Mate?

T. Burke took his feet out of the oven, stretched his legs and put them back again.

"Looks like it might rain again today," he said.

"I think you might be right," said Toddy, squinting expertly through the window at the rain-hill. Then he sat at the table and began to work out a few lines of the Bovo poem. And so they sat out another day surrounded by work that was never going to get done.

Ponto glanced again at the man who'd sat down beside him. The rumpled jacket, the worn-down shoes, the battered little suitcase dropped carelessly by the railway bench.

"Got a light on you, mate?"